MIGUEL DE CERVANTES

EL VIEJO CELOSO AND EL CELOSO EXTREMEÑO

MIGUEL DE CERVANTES

EL VIEJO CELOSO AND
EL CELOSO EXTREMEÑO

EDITED WITH INTRODUCTION,
NOTES & BIBLIOGRAPHY
BY PAUL LEWIS-SMITH

PUBLISHED BY BRISTOL CLASSICAL PRESS
GENERAL EDITOR: JOHN H. BETTS
SPANISH TEXTS SERIES EDITOR: PAUL LEWIS-SMITH

This impression 2002
First published in 2001 by
Bristol Classical Press
an imprint of
Gerald Duckworth & Co. Ltd.
61 Frith Street, London W1D 3JL
Tel: 020 7434 4242
Fax: 020 7434 4420
inquiries@duckworth-publishers.co.uk
www.ducknet.co.uk

A catalogue record for this book is available
from the British Library

ISBN 1 85399 607 6

Printed and bound in Great Britain by
Antony Rowe Ltd, Eastbourne

Cover illustration: 'A Jealous Husband Killing His Wife',
attributed to Titian (*c.* 1485-1576)
reproduced by kind permission of
L'Ecole Nationale Supérieure des Beaux-Arts.

CONTENTS

PREFACE

El viejo celoso and *El celoso extremeño* lend themselves well to comparative study but are related rather than parallel works and differ in their complexity. This edition places the easier text first. The volume as a whole has been prepared for readers who have not previously studied Cervantes or the Golden Age. It is suitable for use at university level in general courses on literature, drama and society in the Golden Age, as well as in courses devoted to Cervantes. I hope that schools will also find it of interest. Attention could be focussed on just one of the works at pre-university level, and the Introduction facilitates such an approach.

The texts are based on the first editions of the collections to which they belong: Cervantes' *Ocho comedias y ocho entremeses* (1615); and his *Novelas ejemplares* (1613). On editorial methods, see p. lxix.

I have benefited from the work of earlier editors from Schevill and Bonilla onwards. I am particularly indebted to their textual notes and am incorporating much of their wisdom in this edition, paring it down in some areas, while, I hope, extending it in others.

Lexical difficulties that have not been dealt with in the textual notes or glossary can be quickly resolved by referring to good modern dictionaries (e.g. the large *Collins* or *Oxford* dictionaries). The short glossary comprises terms that recur in one or both of the works and its purpose is to limit the number of notes and to minimise cross-referencing.

I should like to record my special thanks to Barry Ife, John Lyon and Gordon Minter for their valuable comments on earlier drafts of the Introduction and the notes to the Cervantine texts.

Paul Lewis-Smith
August 2000

KEY TO SHORT REFERENCES

Asensio. Miguel de Cervantes, *Entremeses*, ed. Eugenio Asensio (Madrid: Castalia, 1970).

Avalle-Arce. Miguel de Cervantes, *Novelas ejemplares*, ed. Juan Bautista Avalle-Arce, 3 vols (Madrid: Castalia, 1982), II.

Correas. Gonzalo Correas, *Vocabulario de refranes y frases proverbiales* (c.1630), ed. Louis Combet (Bordeaux: Féret et Fils, 1967).

Covarrubias. Sebastián de Covarrubias, *Tesoro de la lengua castellana o española según la impresión de 1611, con las adiciones de Benito Remigio Noydens publicadas en la de 1674*, ed. Martín de Riquer (Barcelona: Alta Fulla, 1987).

Dic. Aut. Real Academia Española, *Diccionario de autoridades. Edición facsímil*, 3 vols (Madrid: Gredos, 1964). A facsimile edition of the Real Academia's *Diccionario de la lengua castellana* (1726-37).

Forcione. See Selected Bibliography.

Gilbert. See Selected Bibliography.

Granjel. Luis S. Granjel, *Los ancianos en la España de los Austria*, Colección Relectiones, 21 (Salamanca: Universidad Pontificia de Salamanca, 1996).

Hamilton. Earl J. Hamilton, *American Treasure and the Price Revolution in Spain, 1501-1650*, Harvard Economic Studies, 43 (New York: Octagon Books, 1970).

Honig. *Interludes: Miguel de Cervantes*, trans. Edwin Honig (New York: New American Library, 1964).

Molho. Maurice Molho, 'Aproximación al *Celoso extremeño*', *Nueva Revista de Filología Hispánica,* 38 (1990), 743-92.

Molinié-Bertrand. See Selected Bibliography.

Rodríguez Marín. Miguel de Cervantes, *Novelas ejemplares*, ed. Francisco Rodríguez Marín, Clásicos Castellanos, 3 vols (Madrid: Espasa-Calpe, 1965), II.

Schevill and Bonilla. *Obras completas de Miguel de Cervantes Saavedra. Novelas ejemplares*, ed. Rodolfo Schevill and Adolfo Bonilla, 3 vols. (Madrid: Gráficas Reunidas, 1922-5), II.

Thacker. Miguel de Cervantes Saavedra, *Exemplary Novels (Novelas ejemplares)*, General Editor: B.W. Ife, 4 vols (Warminster: Aris and Phillips, 1992), III, with introductions, translations and notes by Michael and Jonathan Thacker.

Williamson. See Selected Bibliography.

Zimic. See Selected Bibliography.

INTRODUCTION

Cervantes: his life, narrative works, and plays

Miguel de Cervantes lived from 1547 to 1616. His career as a writer began around 1582 and continued until the time of his death, with one interruption for a period of about ten years from 1587. His output was broad in range: three long novels of different kinds (*historia* or *libro* was the name for a novel); novellas (*novelas*); full-length plays in verse (*comedias*, standardised as three-act plays in the early 1580s); miniature comedies in prose or verse (*entremeses*); and poems. His strengths lay in narrative fiction and in the miniature comic drama. His most successful work was the novel, *Don Quijote*. This work alone accords him a status in Spanish narrative which is comparable to that of Shakespeare in English drama. The same work probably gives him a global importance as an inspiration for other writers which surpasses that of his English contemporary.

Miguel de Cervantes was never rich and he never held high office. Although technically he belonged to the petty nobility – the *hidalgo* class – he did not come from a family of noble reputation and he probably favoured an ambiguous 'possibly noble' identity in his own social life.[1] In socio-economic terms his origins were very modest. His father had once been a man of means, but had fallen into penury at an early stage in the marriage; his children knew him as a struggling *cirujano*: a 'surgeon'. This term was used for an occupation that was far removed from the modern profession of surgery and much less comfortable and less prestigious than that of a general physician. Surgeons were sometimes barbers, and it is possible that Cervantes' father became involved in this trade.

The Cervantes family led an unsettled life that followed the vagaries of the father's quest for business. Born in Alcalá de Henares, Miguel was taken to Valladolid in north-west Spain, thence south to Andalusia (Córdoba, Cabra, Seville), and in 1566 to Madrid, the growing city adjacent to Alcalá de Henares where Philip II had settled the Court in 1561. His schooling was probably good, though it is likely to have been fitful. He completed it 1568, the year of his twenty-first birthday, at an academy in Madrid.

He did not go on to study at a university. It appears that in 1569 he was prosecuted and severely sentenced *in absentia* for wounding a man in a duel. This brush with the law would have ruined his chances of attending university and it was probably responsible for his departure to Italy at the end of the same year. The move to Italy must have played an important part in Cervantes' formation as a writer. Like most progressive Spanish writers of the same generation, he was deeply influenced by the literary and intellectual achievement of the Italian Renaissance, and it was doubtless during his stay in Italy that he began his deeper acquaintance with that achievement. But the Italian period was first and foremost a life adventure, not a literary one. For a short time he lived in Rome, where he worked for an Italian cardinal in a minor household position. He then moved south to Naples (which was Spanish territory at this time) and enlisted in the Spanish army. The major event in his military career was the naval Battle of Lepanto (1571) in which Spain and her allies inflicted a crucial defeat on the Ottoman Turks. He distinguished himself by his bravery in this engagement. Despite being ill, he insisted on taking part in the battle and fought to exhaustion having suffered serious wounds, including one which permanently maimed his left hand and arm. Lepanto was one of the vivid memories that he used in the early 1580s to bridge the gulf between the previous ten years of his life, adrenalin-filled and justifiably regarded as heroic years by his modern biographers, with the occupation of writing. *La batalla naval*, the title of one of his lost early plays, clearly alludes to Lepanto.

In 1575 he took ship to return Spain. Carrying high-level testimonials to his exemplary conduct in Italy, he was probably hoping to obtain an executive or secretarial position in the Spanish civil service; but his immediate future was very different from whatever he might have planned. His ship became one of the many European vessels to be captured in the Mediterranean by Muslim pirates who operated from North Africa. As the consequence of this misfortune he spent the next five years of his life as a prisoner in Algiers. There he joined thousands of other Christians who had fallen into Muslim hands through warfare, piracy and raids on coasts and islands in the Mediterranean. These unfortunate men and women were condemned to slavery unless their families were able to arrange their ransom. In Cervantes' case, the prestigious testimonials that had been found on his person worked against him by causing his captors to price his freedom at a level that was beyond the family's resources. This helps to explain why he repeatedly placed his life at risk by attempting to escape to Spain or to the Spanish redoubt of Orán, before he was finally released. Freedom unexpectedly arrived in 1580 when his family had secured the funds they lacked from the Trinitarian Friars, a religious order that devoted itself to the cause of rescuing captives from Algiers.

Back in Spain, he made unsuccessful attempts to gain entry to the civil service. With the most powerful of his military patrons now dead and with no great influence inside the bureaucratic establishment, he was offered only a temporary appointment that took him back to North Africa, where he was required to report on the defensive position of Orán. Rejected for a civil-service career, by 1582 he had settled into literary life in the Spanish capital and was producing his first book: *La Galatea*, a pastoral romance that was published in 1585.[2] At about the same time he launched himself as a playwright. His first play was probably a very 'committed' drama about captive life in Algiers, entitled *El trato de Argel*. This is one of just two examples which have survived from the twenty to thirty *comedias* he later claimed he had written in this period. It is a reasonable conjecture that he also wrote *entremeses* during these years.

The major event in his private life in this period was his marriage in 1584 with Catalina de Palacios, a nineteen-year-old whose family lived in Esquivias, a village in the province of Toledo. Cervantes reaped little profit from his marriage. Whilst the family possessed substantial assets in the form of land and property, in cash terms they lived on the edge of insolvency; Catalina's dowry was therefore paltry; and it was handed over late (1586). These economic facts together with the brief duration of the couple's courtship, which lasted a mere three months, strongly suggest that the marriage sealed a romance. However, the groom's feelings towards his bride may well have been naïvely prejudiced by a growing disillusionment with the life that he was leading in Madrid. His restlessness perhaps owed something to a certain psychological need of moral self-purification, for at the time of his wedding he had only just ended a sexual relationship with a married woman called Ana de Villafranca, who bore him a daughter shortly after his wedding.[3] Whatever his motivations were, the marriage was a disappointment. In 1587, not three years after taking his vows, Cervantes virtually suspended it, having clearly undergone a deep personal crisis.

In that year, his fortieth, he turned his back on his married, literary and theatrical lives and uprooted to Andalusia. There he secured by prior arrangement a nomadic job requisitioning supplies for the navy, which was then preparing for the Armada (1588). He later became a collector of taxes working in the same region. He did not return from southern Spain on a permanent basis until 1600 or 1601. By that time he had ceased to work for the Spanish government and was surviving somehow in Seville, the city in which he had begun his Andalusian career and where he had undergone a period of imprisonment for mismanaging his tax affairs (1597). It must have ben there, probably between about 1596 and the turn of the century, that he rediscovered his vocation for writing and began the mental readjustments that would take him back to Madrid, the political, literary and theatrical capital of Spain. An early version of *El celoso extremeño* can safely be assigned to this transitional period, and it was probably in the same period that *Don Quijote* began to take form.

The years between his return from Andalusia and the time of his death were Cervantes' most productive. Throughout these years writing was his sole occupation and for the most part he lived in Madrid, now reunited with his wife.[4] His first publication in this period was Part I of *Don Quijote* (*El ingenioso hidalgo don Quijote de la Mancha*), which appeared in 1605. It instantly became a best-seller in Spain and was soon acclaimed abroad. A second Part appeared in 1615. *Don Quijote* is by common consent the supreme achievement in early modern narrative. Whilst revealing an author of great versatility, essentially it is a comic work on a theme that is particularly characteristic of Cervantes' output in the Andalusian and post-Andalusian years: *engaño*, a theme that ranges from comic deception to tragic self-delusion, and whose precise significance is mercurial. Tragic versions of the *engaño* theme occur amongst the secondary tales that are incorporated in *Don Quijote*. Here, however, it is fundamentally a humorous theme that grows naturally out of Cervantes' intention of parodying 'books of chivalry': *libros de caballerías*. Books of chivalry were heroic tales that had originated in the Middle Ages and which purported to be true accounts of the adventures of illustrious knights who had lived in bygone times.[5] In reality they were heroic romances, and the adventures they recounted were neither true nor possible. Their extreme lack of verisimilitude had discredited them by rational standards at the end of the sixteenth century;[6] yet they still possessed a certain charm and simple people still tended to confuse them with fact – or so Cervantes implies. With *Don Quijote* he accelerated the decline of the genre by transforming rational views of it into lifelike comic fiction. Realistically set in contemporary Spain, the novel depicts an obsessive reader of books of chivalry whose addiction to them so blights his brain that he takes them as the true stories they claim to be, and vaingloriously attempts to emulate their heroes. Hoping that he too will become the subject of a *libro de caballerías*, he seeks out chivalresque adventures in a real world that can only hold up for ridicule both him and books of chivalry – him as a madman, them as implausible lies.

Cervantes' other narrative works were a serious contribution to heroic romance – *Los trabajos de Persiles y Sigismunda*, a work inspired by Classical models that was posthumously published in 1617 – and a varied collection of extended short stories which competed with those of the Italian *novellieri*. These tales, the *Novelas ejemplares* (1613), from which *El celoso extremeño* is taken, are now his most admired achievement after *Don Quijote*.

In the 1580s Cervantes appears to have put most of his energy into writing for the public theatres. In later life – almost certainly post-Andalusian life – he continued to write *comedias*; but competition from younger playwrights under the gifted leadership of Lope de Vega (1562-1635), and concomitant adjustments of fashion, conspired to make him *persona non grata* with the directors of the acting companies who purchased plays for performance. We owe the survival of his later *comedias*, together with that of his *entremeses*, to a deal that he made with a minor publisher towards the end of his life. The result of this deal was the dramatic collection in which *El viejo celoso* first appeared: the *Ocho comedias y ocho entremeses nuevos, nunca representados* (1615).[7] As its title implies and as Cervantes makes perfectly clear in the Prologue, this volume was intended to preserve the plays in the hope that they would one day be performed.

In the Prologue to the collection of plays the *entremeses* barely receive a mention. This authorial modesty is a poor guide to their quality as comic drama. Modern critics rightly describe them as minor masterpieces. They are reminiscent of the comic genius on display in greater depth and breadth in the set-piece conversational episodes and action 'dramas' that fill the pages of Cervantes' most famous novel, *Don Quijote*. Their author's casual attitude towards them is partly explained by their brevity (they are long as *entremeses* go but are within the customary limits), and partly by the lowliness of *entremeses* in the hierarchy of contemporary genres and by their related role in the theatre. In a narrative and dramatic culture that notionally accorded status to works in the light of the social, sentimental and moral dignity of their subject-matter and the elevation of their language, the *entremés* was a 'humble' genre, ranking therefore beneath conventional *comedias*. The latter were either romantic comedies set in genteel social worlds or were hybrid plays by Classical standards (i.e. tragicomedies) that normally ended happily but whose basic tone was serious and heroic. A good *comedia* was elegantly poetic. The *entremés* was a short, boisterous, unsentimental form of comedy. Its characters were always unheroic and unromantic, its social environment was common, and it cultivated a style of humour that was less decorous than that of romantic comedy and altogether more merry. Accordingly it was not a poetic genre, though by 1615 it was well on the way to abandoning prose in preference for verse.[8] The qualities of *entremeses* are explained by the essentially ludic nature of the role they fulfilled in the theatre. Their routine function, reflected in the name *entremés*, was that of providing light refreshment between the first and second acts at performances of *comedias*. Covarrubias gives the classic definition of the genre in his dictionary of 1611:

Entremés. Está corrompido del italiano *intremeso*, que vale tanto como entremetido o enjerido, y es propiamente una representación de risa y graciosa que se entremete entre un acto y otro de la comedia, para alegrar y espaciar al auditorio.[9]

The customary role of the *entremés* in the contemporary theatre explains the numerical composition of Cervantes' volume of plays. The *ocho entremeses* are self-evidently offered as interlude pieces for the *ocho comedias*. It is a safe conjecture that they never served that purpose, for we may safely assume that the *comedias* were never staged. However, we cannot rule out the possibility that *El viejo celoso* and other *entremeses* reached the stage as interlude pieces that graced *comedias* written by other hands. Given that Cervantes was known to the public as the author of a hugely funny novel, there would clearly have been a box-office case for using his *entremeses* in this way.

Cultural introduction to *El viejo celoso* and *El celoso extremeño*

El viejo celoso and *El celoso extremeño* are both examples of Cervantes' interest in the theme of *engaño* and are rare examples of works by him with very similar plots. They even have heroes with very similar names: 'Cañizares' in the *entremés* and 'Felipo de Carrizales' in the novella. Both works deal with a naïvely irresponsible marriage which founders upon the conflicting needs of the spouses – Cañizares and Lorenza in the *entremés*, Carrizales and Leonora in the novella. The core problems are age differentials between the partners and jealousy on the part of the husband. In each work the wife is a teenage girl from a poor or very modest background and the husband is an elderly man of means. Wealth is the thing that enables the *viejo* to acquire his bride in *El celoso extremeño* and that has enabled him to do so in the *entremés*, where the wedding is an event in the past. Lorenza in the *entremés* was fifteen when she married Cañizares, who had passed the age of seventy, and the apparent age of Leonora is thirteen or fourteen when she marries Carrizales, who at the time is sixty-eight. Each of the husbands is attacked by jealousy once he obtains his bride. This is jealousy not in the sense of envy, but in the older sense of a zealous or intense possessiveness (e.g. the 'jealous' God of the Old Testament is possessive towards His chosen people) which involves distrust and anxiety when the jealousy is that of a husband. In Cervantes' works it impels the husband to place his wife in a kind of gilded cage. Her home becomes a luxurious prison which excludes all other masculinity (human or animal) and is meant to suppress her sexuality and the interest of younger men. In each work the security measures fail. The basic differences between the two plots lie in the form of the sexual conspiracy that takes place behind the husband's back and in what happens to the marriage, which chiefly depends on the moral character of the wife. The marriage in the *entremés* becomes a source of hilarity when a wily wife who takes a lover successfully pretends that her unfaithfulness is an illusion. In the novella, the marriage becomes a domestic catastrophe when an ingenuous wife who is tempted by a sexual predator succeeds, just, in preserving her virtue, only to be caught in a situation that convinces the husband of her guilt. Both these works revolve around eccentric examples of a type of marriage that was known as *matrimonio desigual*. Although such marriage was not the norm in contemporary Spain, in more moderate forms it is likely to have been quite common. Cervantes depicts more moderate forms in other works with Spanish settings[10] and he himself contracted a marriage that was moderately *desigual*, his bride being almost twenty years his junior. Age differentials of this magnitude were commended by clerical moralists. The latter believed that procreation was the essential purpose of married life and that moderately 'unequal' marriage was ideally suited to the task of rearing children.[11] Cervantes' outlook was probably very different. He evidently believed that sexual love was an essential ingredient in an ideal marriage and he nowhere promoted a romantic ideal of married life in which the partners belonged to widely different age-groups. It is a reasonable assumption that he learnt a lesson from his own matrimonial experience. However, in the works that we are examining here he is attacking only *matrimonio desigual* in an extreme form that was generally condemned. No one believed that men should marry once they had reached old age. Father Juan de Pineda, a well-known clerical moralist who firmly believed in an age-inequality of up to twenty years, was airing contemporary common-sense when he disqualified men who were old, bluntly declaring: 'Los viejos no son para casados. Matrimonio, huye de la vejez.'[12] Cervantes, furthermore, positions his heroes well beyond the threshold of old age. Whilst male old age normally began at sixty or later in traditional scholarly theories of age (Granjel, pp. 13-25), in intuitive perceptions of age it arrived at a much earlier stage in life. When Juan de Pineda and most other people thought of 'los viejos', they included men who today would not be considered old and would not be discouraged from marrying and rearing children. In the real world a man of forty was probably at the threshold of old age.[13] A woman was probably growing old when she reached her middle thirties.[14] To understand the period's intuitions of age the modern reader must bear in mind that sixty was a ripe old age by contemporary standards of life expectancy, that people literally aged more quickly in the absence of advanced medical care, and that the concept of a 'middle' age had not yet taken form. A person was old when he or she had patently ceased to be young in physical terms.

Cañizares and Carrizales are therefore *very* old men. This, however, is not to say that the age-inequalities in Cervantes' works are wildly impossible by contemporary social standards. In both works the girlish age of the imprisoned bride is perfectly consistent with the customs of marriage in the sixteenth and seventeenth centuries. Many girls were married off in their middle teens and the minimum age at which a girl could legally marry was twelve. Hence the proverb: 'No es poco ser casada y tener moco' (Correas, p. 247b).[15] The role of parental or other authority in arranging the marriage on the bride's side is also true to life.[16] Both true to life and significant as social comment are the material values that justify the marriage in the eyes of her parents or guardian, and which the bride herself embraced in the *entremés*. The power of money is one of the more distinctive themes in Spanish literature of Cervantes' period and it includes the theme of avaricious marriage, the profit motive usually lying on the woman's side of the match. One motif is that of money-minded parents who impose their values on innocent daughters, whilst another is that of the worldly young woman who herself puts money first. The novella is a version of the first motif, whilst the two motifs converge in the *entremés*. Both appear as separate motifs in other works by Cervantes.[17]

A satirical passage in a contemporary work by another writer, Salas Barbadillo, is of special interest to us here. This is a passage that links female greed with *matrimonio desigual* and attests the reality of 'inequalities' which are almost as grotesque as those depicted in the novella and the *entremés*. It is only as regards the brides, who are evidently more mature young women than their Cervantine fictional counterparts, that differences seem to exist. In the passage in question the speaker is reporting the decrees of a judge who is prosecuting madness:

Declara...por hombres menguados de seso a los que siendo muy viejos y ricos se casan, dando por causa el deseo de la sucesión cuando están más inútiles para ella, porque estos tales son de sus mujeres ayos y no maridos, [y] viven siempre acechando sus celos...También quiere que sean comprendidas en el mismo número las mujeres gallardas y mozas que se casan con ellos a título de heredallos.[18]

The marriages that Salas Barbadillo describes are entirely made by money. The wives are interested in becoming rich widows by inheriting their husbands' estates, whilst the husbands are intent on acquiring their own legitimate offspring on whom to settle their wealth, though they are unlikely to achieve their ambitions. The hero of *El celoso extremeño* is a husband of this kind. What chiefly differentiates him within the class of *viejo* husband that Salas Barbadillo describes is his possession of aristocratic rank, the fact that he is a very jealous man by inborn disposition ('natural condición' [p. 20]), and the crucial role that sexual infatuation plays in swaying him into marriage. As a naturally very jealous man he quakes at the thought of getting married and abandons the idea until he has set eyes on Leonora. He then needs to tranquillise his jealous nature by convincing himself that her childish age will allow him to dominate her. His success in calming his jealousy is a sign of how much he desires Leonora and is a cautionary example of that form of delusion that we now call wishful thinking, of which there are numerous examples in this novella. But there is also a cultural significance in this episode. It reflects a morally contemptuous view of aristocratic attitudes to marriage. It suggests that social pride and greed are the motives that determine the typical marriage in the aristocratic class. A subsidiary aspect of Carrizales' infatuation is his failure to wonder if Leonora is aristocratic or common. When her parents turn out to be aristocratic and delay assent to his request for her hand until they have checked his social credentials, whilst inviting Carrizales to check their own, Cervantes is driving home the point that aristocrats normally married within their own social class. A shrewd reader would doubtless have sensed that he was obliquely condemning wealthy nobles for contracting marriage for the sole purpose of preserving their family lines and wealth by siring children on women of suitable stock. His main targets were probably men in the higher, titled aristocracy, as distinct from mere *hidalgos*. Carrizales is easily a millionaire (in modern sterling terms). In real life, a suitor as rich as Carrizales would probably have been a higher noble who had inherited his title and large estate from his late father and was seeking a wife because he now needed to produce his own successor.[19] A further thrust at the noble classes is the portrait of aristocratic parents who are content to give their daughter away to her ancient suitor provided that he too is aristocratic. This alludes simultaneously to the excessive social power of money and to aristocratic prejudice against it when it is owned by commoners. Cervantes is thinking of noble but impoverished parents who turn down offers for their daughters' hands from prosperous men of common class for no reason other than snobbery. Though probably not implausible for a contemporary readership, the snobbery of Leonora's parents is no less extreme than the economic ruthlessness with which they accept the suitor's offer when they are certain of his noble rank.

Cañizares in the *entremés* is different from Carrizales in the novella. Firstly, he is a common man married to a common woman. Secondly, he did not get married because he wanted bloodline heirs to whom he would leave his estate. He may well have known that he was incapable of siring them, unlike Carrizales, who possesses a feeble potency that allows him to delude himself. Thirdly, he is not a man with a jealous nature who married a fifteen year-old girl because he wanted a wife he could dominate. Rather, he is an ordinary man who wanted a caring and congenial companion in the winter of his life, had a sentimental weakness for girls, like all old men, so this work suggests

(p. 3), and virtually equated a teenage wife with an attentive and charming daughter. Although they are perfectly plausible ones, the motives that Cañizares is given for marrying Lorenza are probably determined by the conventions of *entremeses*. Like his unaristocratic rank, they are consistent with levity. They make him less unlikeable than the rich old man who marries in order to generate heirs, and they distance him still further from the married nobility. His significance as a cautionary character is less impudent than that of Carrizales and is much more centred on his age and his jealousy, the second of which, being entirely explicable in the light of his age and his impotence, is that of a 'typical' husband who is very old.

El viejo celoso conforms to a stereotypical view of the kinds of problem that naturally lay in store for *viejos* if they decided to marry *mozas*. The novella is an adaptation of the same view. Infidelity on the wife's part and jealousy on the husband's part were well-known fruits of such marriages. According to a scabrous proverb, a *viejo* who was stupid enough to wed a young woman must either be cuckolded or wind up dead from sexual over-exertion: 'Viejo que con moza casó, o muere cabrito, o vive cabrón' (Correas, p. 521a).[20] Salas Barbadillo links old age with jealousy ('viven siempre acechando sus celos') and Father Juan de Pineda expects the *viejo* to be jealous. A Jesuit account of a crime of passion that obscurely took place in Madrid in 1646 sheds some anecdotal light on the real dangers that lay behind these stereotypical warnings. A woman whom the report describes as 'moza y de no mal arte' (young and attractive) who was married to an 'hombre viejo' was unfaithful to her husband. This caused the death of an innocent man when the husband made a confused attempt to avenge the *agravio* (Granjel, p. 110).

Jealousy, however, was not an ailment peculiar to husbands who had married in their old age. It may have been a frequent male complaint. Cultural conditions were certainly more conducive to it than those which prevail today. Though a marriage could not be dissolved by divorce, the romantic marriage was less common and the marriage of social and economic convenience may well have been the norm. This helps to explain why the law permitted a married man to keep a mistress provided he did not parade her. To make matters worse still, a man's *honor* – his respectability and, by extension, his entitlement to self-esteem – was widely felt to depend upon the chastity of his women (wife, daughters, and any unmarried sisters). By contrast, a man's *own* sexual behaviour affected his honour very little; the main danger for a man who seduced another's wife was the possibility that the husband would take revenge. In such a world, a husband who was not convinced of his wife's instinctive loyalty towards him and who knew that his social position was weak – that rivals might not be frightened of him, or that he lacked the means of protecting his interests – would inevitably have suffered from jealousy, if he shared or feared the conventional prejudices. The most naked displays of male angst in the period's culture as we see it today lie in its store of proverbs, which chiefly speak for the lower social orders. 'Don't flash your wallet or your woman', might be a suitable modern version of one proverb that directly expresses a fear of sexual predators: 'Espada y mujer, ni darlas a ver' (Correas, p. 149b).[21] Another proverb, this one clearly of rural origin, reflects upon the vexing problem for men in the lower social classes of keeping female property under 'guard': 'Mujer hermosa, niña e higueral, muy malos son de guardar.'[22] Another piece of homely wisdom is representative of the unabashed misogynism that sometimes appears in proverbs: 'En la vida, la mujer tres salidas ha de hacer: al bautismo, al casamiento, a la sepultura o monumento.'[23] Nastier still is the following proverb, in which we hear the voice of the bully: 'La mujer casada y honrada, la pierna quebrada y en casa; y la doncella, pierna y media.'[24]

The worried husband must have been a good deal rarer in the social class to which Carrizales belongs than in the lower classes whose voices we hear in proverbs. The wealthy nobility had many reasons for feeling that they were secure: they possessed social prestige and power; their homes were private, well-staffed, and luxurious; their wives came from good stock; and they were under the guard of matronly chaperones. Cervantes himself is well aware that husbands in the wealthy nobility are not ordinarily jealous in the anxious way that is natural in other men. As an elderly husband who by inborn nature, let alone age, is 'the most jealous man in the world' (p. 20), the apprehensive Carrizales is clearly conceived as a special case within his social class. Cervantes, however, uses him on one level as a convenient means of obliquely accusing a normal husband in the same class of marital complacency. This ulterior social motive is partly detectable as a disruptive influence on his account of Carrizales' attitude towards his own married life. He is attributed at different times with the continuing anxiety to be expected of a pathologically jealous man and with the self-satisfaction to be expected of a man who is not neurotically apprehensive, but complacently naïve.

Where Cervantes' ulterior motivation is most apparent is in the role that he gives to the *dueña* Marialonso, who is the weakest link in Carrizales' defences, and in the slanderous comment that he gleefully passes on Marialonso's profession. *Dueñas* were older and single women whose main employers were the rich nobility and who were entrusted with two tasks: chaperoning wives and daughters, and supervising other female servants. Cervantes was not the first writer to give them a bad press. Despite being the highest occupational level a woman could reach, their profession was not a prestigious one, and writers with an impertinent bent were fond of insulting it. They depicted *dueñas* as stupid, tiresome, and at worst as hypocrites.

Marialonso is an extreme version of the hypocrite: a *dueña* who acts as a go-between in an illicit sexual relationship. She actually becomes a procuress, thus taking on the moral identity of a kind of female whose social role was the opposite of that of a *dueña*. It is impossible to tell to what extent *dueñas* deserved their reputations and to what extent they were glibly slandered by men who disliked the class they served, or disliked women who wielded a certain social authority over the male sex; but the tradition that lies behind the character must be borne in mind when considering Marialonso. She is doubtless intended to please the reader by carrying the tradition from which she springs to still more cynical heights. It is likely that she is also conceived as a mockery of cultural isolation on the part of the rich nobility. The satire of *dueñas* was concentrated in more popular genres with which the Spanish upper-class would not have been very familiar.[25] The crucial naïvety of Carrizales is his ignorance of this class-related mockery of *dueñas*. The hypocritical Marialonso appears to be 'de mucha prudencia y graveded' (p. 22) and Carrizales does not doubt that she is.

At the point at which the *dueña* becomes Loaysa's procuress, Cervantes fires two emotional tirades against *dueñas* as a breed. It is these tirades that fully reveal to the modern reader his malevolence towards the rich and aristocratic husbands for whom they typically worked. In both of them the narrator's voice is ironically histrionic. He engages in deliberate over-statement or 'irony of excess'. In the first tirade he underlines his ironic intention by addressing one of his mock-indignant apostrophes to the *dueñas'* headdresses (*tocas*). Here we are dealing with a deliberate form of bathos – a sudden and comic descent in style – that involves a burlesque form of metonym, a manner of speaking in which the part denotes the whole (*tocas* stands for *dueñas*). Here are the passages in the order in which they occur:

¡Oh dueñas, nacidas y usadas en el mundo para perdición de mil recatadas y buenas intenciones! ¡Oh luengas y repulgadas tocas, escogidas para autorizar las salas y los estrados de señoras principales! ¡Y cuán al revés de lo que debíades usáis de vuestro casi ya forzoso oficio! (p. 40)

Libre Dios a cada uno de tales enemigos, contra los cuales no hay escudo de prudencia que defienda ni espada de recato que corte. (p. 41)

Both are examples of *el hablar equívoco* (ambivalent speech), a device much favoured in contemporary *comedias* as a source of what we now call 'dramatic' irony, which occurs when the speaker, the character addressed, or both parties are unconscious of the ambivalence. Here we are dealing with something very similar to dramatic irony. In each passage the author and his readers are jeering at a wealthy nobleman behind the nobleman's back, enjoying the thought of a *dueña* betraying him. At the same time they are probably jeering at naïvety – thinking of him as a man like Carrizales, who presumed that *dueñas* could be trusted. The second passage is the more typical and subtle example of *el hablar equívoco*, since it adds to the histrionic irony of mock indignation an ambivalent imagery that belittles aristocratic status and money. This irony of verbal double-meaning is located in the second half of the statement, 'no hay escudo de prudencia que defienda ni espada de recato que corte', and lies in the emblematic sense of the word *espada* and the multivalent range of *escudo*. The sword is a metonymic emblem of noble rank, whilst the word *escudo* alludes to both nobility and wealth. It ironically means three things: 'shield'; 'coat of arms'; and *escudo* in the sense of a gold coin that bore the arms of the monarch.

The novella is quite strongly influenced by its setting in Seville, the place in which it originated. The fact that it assumes no inside knowledge of Sevillian society shows that Cervantes wrote it with publication as his ultimate goal. However, we know that he first released it in the 1590s in manuscript form to a public in Seville. Furthermore the style in which the tale is narrated has elements of conversational speech, performative features, like the tirades against *dueñas*, and other qualities that suggest that he wrote it as much with oral delivery in mind as circulation to groups of readers. At one point (p. 23) he actually refers to an audience, using a phrase, 'como ahora oiréis', which originates in the narrative style of medieval works that were composed for oral delivery before the introduction of printing. The likelihood that he was most consciously addressing a private public when he wrote the novella helps to explain its social exclusivism. On one level it is an anti-aristocratic text at the centre of which is an oblique attack on wealthy nobles who marry for reasons of convenience. As originally written, it may have been an attack on the Sevillian nobility in particular. All in all it slights the intelligence of the wealthy nobility and it assaults both their tranquillity and their *honor*, for Cervantes evidently relishes the idea of such men being cuckolded. In conception, however, the attack on the aristocratic husband is symbolic rather than real. Although the novella may well have been read by husbands whom it obliquely lampoons, it is mentally located in a social space from which these men are excluded, or are excluded for most of the time. It is only the ending which contains some evidence of an author who consciously includes such men in the public for which he is writing. The wife who at the eleventh hour refrains from committing adultery is a modified version of a heroine who in the original and unpublished draft, written in Seville in the late 1590s, is in fact seduced.[26] Cervantes may have altered his heroine in a way that made her a morally more respectable figure partly in order to make the novella less impudent towards the wealthy nobility when he had become more conscious of the broader public he would reach through publication, having originally drafted the tale with a limited public of Sevillian acquaintances uppermost in his mind, or having conceived its satirical implications with this limited public in mind.

Though the setting of the novella is Seville, the hero's place of birth was Extremadura. Carrizales' *extremeño* background can be explained in various ways. It is possibly influenced by a folklore of regional character-traits in which Extremadurans were stereotyped as jealous (Molho, pp. 746-7). Cervantes may have engaged this tradition in order to give greater plausibility to his fictional portrait of a pathologically jealous husband who is aristocratic and rich. The hero's Extremaduran origins may also be construed as witty. It is possible for the word *extremeño* to acquire the meaning *extremado* from the trait of extremeness that is one of three overlapping traits which permeate the hero's character as it unfolds, the others being materialism and a 'straightforward' or *llano* intelligence.[27] Two things can be said with certainty: that the hero's territorial background should not be seen as the essential aspect of his social identity; and that it is instrumental in his characterisation as a man who is lost to sin. Carrizales is first and foremost a very wealthy nobleman whose regional origin helps to stress that men of his kind are lacking in Christian charity. The outstanding example of this moral flaw is the attitude he adopts towards the notorious poverty of his native region on returning from the Indies as a millionaire. Considering that his penurious neighbours would be likely to disturb his peace and quiet by pestering him for money, he thinks better of spending his retirement in Extremadura (p. 20).

Cuckoldry in fiction: Cervantes and literary tradition

Though each of these works is in some degree a satire of contemporary life and manners, the initial inspiration for them comes from earlier works of fiction and not from life in the raw. Cervantes was building on a traditional kind of matrimonial tale. As the story ran in its usual form, an old and socially powerful man married a young and beautiful woman, despotically tried to secure her loyalty (e.g. by locking her in a tower), but ended up being cuckolded all the same. This type of tale appears to have pandered to the sexual frustrations of young men who could not compete in the marriage market with mature men who were well established in life. It chiefly flourished in Renaissance Italy, where social as well as literary conditions favoured its propagation.[28] It was probably from Italy that Cervantes took his cue. A likely source of inspiration is Matteo Boiardo's *Orlando innamorato*, a late fifteenth-century romance of chivalry which manages to thread the tale tradition into its narrative weave. The husband in the Boiardan version is a rich man of more than sixty years of age whose neurotic traits and deceitfulness arc very reminiscent of the heroes of Cervantes' two works.[29] But he could have read many similar tales in Renaissance novella collections, including much more humorous versions than the one in Boiardo's romance. Matteo Bandello is the most likely source of inspiration amongst the Italian *novellieri* and one of his stories almost certainly played an important role in the genesis of the *entremés*. This work shows signs of a special debt to Bandello's tale of how the wily wife Bindoccia deceives her jealous husband Angravalle.[30]

Husband-deception may have been a familiar motif in sixteenth-century *entremeses*, but *El viejo celoso* is likely to have been a very distinctive version of it by the standards of the genre[31] and it is not a slavish adaptation of the story told by Bandello. Angravalle, for example, is forty-something, not in his seventies like Cañizares, and the trick that is played upon him is less ingenious than the trick that is played by Lorenza. The Cervantine piece is nonetheless a conservative treatment of the traditional formula carried out in the jovial style that the *novellieri* tended to favour. *El celoso extremeño* is a more serious treatment and a much more innovative one. Its originality chiefly lies in its subordination of comic action revolving around motifs of deception and gullibility to tragic action that is founded upon a misunderstanding and is rich in moral irony. The lover is now a cunning and callous predator and the wife is no longer the wily wildcat to be found in the merrier Italian novellas but a recalcitrant version of the more passive, unworldly and aristocratic adulteresses who generally appear in the more dignified versions of the tradition. Essentially she is an *ingénue* (a female equivalent of Carrizales, in a different way) who plays into the hands of a disguised seducer and reacts too late against sexual temptation to avoid a domestic disaster. She controls her sexual instincts; but she does so at the last minute, when she has gone to bed with the young man, and deceptive appearances reinforced by the husband's propensity to assume the worst, and by the imprudent assumptions of her parents, convict her of the sexual crime from which she has recoiled. Before he dies from the shock of what he believes to have been his wife's adultery, the husband is sufficiently chastened to acknowledge that the age discrepancy between the spouses was the root cause of what he thinks he has discovered. Shouldering the blame, he instructs his wife in his official Will to remarry herself to her lover, the sensually named Loaysa. Leonora, however, rejects this aspect of her husband's Will and chooses to enter a convent. As 'uno de los más recogidos monasterios de la ciudad' (p. 45), the convent is an authentic version of the convent-like fortress in which she had been kept by her husband. The dejected Loaysa, whose disappointment presumably stems from dashed hopes of laying his hands on Leonora's inheritance, disappears to the Indies, as Carrizales had done in his late forties after squandering the wealth he had inherited from his parents.

This ending is the one major change that Cervantes made between drafting the novella in Seville in the later 1590s and submitting it for publication in Madrid in 1612. In the original ending the heroine fully succumbs to Loaysa's advances, Carrizales dies of shock, the heroine retires to a convent in fulfilment of a remorseful promise that she made to him as he was dying; and Loaysa goes off to join the army, where he comes to a sticky end that Cervantes describes as his punishment. Though Cervantes' purpose in changing this ending may have been influenced by fear of the socially powerful class that the novella attacks, the result is not merely an ending that is less impudent towards that class; the revised ending is more surprising, more elegant in structural terms and better attuned to the novella's deeper themes. Whatever else it is designed to achieve, it is undoubtedly intended to produce a superior climax.

Essentially it is an ironical version of the early ending that builds on the theme of *engaño*. Though he may not have done so consciously, Cervantes could have found inspiration for it in the climax of the *entremés*, which chronologically was probably written between the two versions of the novella.[32] Reduced to their bare essentials, the ending of the revised novella and the climax of the *entremés* are contrasting versions of the same essential formula: the one is a mirror-image of the other. The differences lie in the contrast of moods and in the contrasting forms of *engaño*: in one work the husband is deceived by a false appearance of innocence; in the other he is deceived by a false appearance of guilt.

Sex, adultery, and the morality of Cervantes' works

Albeit less aggressively than it did in its original form, in its final form *El celoso extremeño* continues to harbour malicious feelings towards the matrimonial honour of a certain class of husband. However, this ill will is never more than a counter-current of subversive emotion in a text whose author is rationally committed to Christian standards of sexual morality, and who tends to identify the temporal better interests of wives, let alone their spiritual welfare, with unconditional chastity. Cervantes' Christian sensibilities were sharpened no doubt by the laws of censorship. Since adultery was a capital sin, violating the seventh Commandment and the sacramental status of marriage, the religious censors of the Spanish Counter-Reformation would not have assented to the publication of a work that seriously condoned it.[33] Cervantes, in fact, not only condemns it from a Christian perspective but also depicts it as potentially dangerous for wives whose husbands cared deeply about marital honour. This danger is shown in Carrizales' reaction when he thinks he has been betrayed. His behaviour confirms that his jealousy owes less to the possessive affection he feels for his wife than to a deep-seated need of respect from a female partner. It is an extreme example of the violent response that this kind of fetish supposedly justified if a catastrophe occurred in the context of a married relationship. His vengeful reaction of wanting to kill his wife and her lover is unacceptable from an enlightened Christian point of view, but legitimate from the viewpoint of *honor*. The code of honour entitled a husband whose wife had committed adultery to resort to such instant and bloody vengeance as a way of repairing his dignity. Such action, moreover, was legal.[34] What gives the hero a lunatic quality at this point in the tale is his thought of killing not just the lovers, but everyone under his roof.

El celoso extremeño not only adopts a cautionary approach to the subject of female infidelity but also eschews the indecency that was a notorious vice of the Italian *novellieri*.[35] There are no intimate descriptions of human bodies, no probing accounts of erotic fantasies, and apart from brief euphemistic references to matrimonial intercourse, there is only one sexual act: Loaysa's unsuccessful attempt to have intercourse with Leonora. This is recorded in a single sentence whose imagery dignifies the heroine's struggle and conceals all physical detail:

Pero, con todo esto, el valor de Leonora fue tal que en el tiempo que más le convenía, lo mostró [mostró su valor] contra las fuerzas villanas de su astuto engañador, pues no fueron bastantes a vencerla, y él se cansó en balde, y ella quedó vencedora, y entrambos dormidos.   (p. 41)

The sexual morality of the *entremés* is relaxed by comparison with that of the novella, but is not without its standards. The dialogue is peppered with smutty jokes and the comic climax revolves around an unfaithful wife's deception of her husband. However, Cervantes does not mix humour with prurience, he stops short of depicting adultery, and he implies no serious disrespect for the authority of the marriage vows. The jokes are obscenely witty in style rather than sexually provocative, the wife's adventure takes place in private, out of sight of the audience, and there is no suggestion that the couple have sexual intercourse – which was, and still is, the essential ingredient in an adulterous relationship, both by Christian definition and from the viewpoint of secular law.[36] As we shall presently see, the climax of the *entremés* builds upon a comic mechanism that was typical of the genre. By implication it is not intended as an incitement to mismarried wives to form illicit relationships, but merely as a humorous form of moral truancy whose psychological space is the realm of harmless sentiment. In this sense it is comparable to the sexual malice that informs *El celoso extremeño*. In as far as Cervantes is guilty of adopting immoral attitudes to marriage, his sins are like the adultery that is committed in 'el pensamiento' by the heroine of the novella: they are venial sins of 'thought'.

Entremés del viejo celoso

The humour of *El viejo celoso* ranges up from the more physical types that we tend to call farce and slapstick, through the insult-hurling that is the verbal equivalent of slapstick, to the sophisticated, more intelligent humour of irony and wit. Its comic climax reflects a preference for intelligent humour and is a clever version of the comic device on which most *entremeses* were based: the *burla*, a trick or practical joke. This formula was used in Italian comic novellas (*burla* = Italian *beffa*) but was directly inherited from the *paso*, an embryonic *entremés* that consisted of a comic digression *inside* a full-length play, as distinct from an interlude performed between the acts. The *burla* in *El viejo celoso* interlaces a simple trick of a kind that the audience is primed to expect, the smuggling of a young man into the house and out again beneath the nose of Cañizares, with a subtle and unexpected trick which transfers the role of arch-deceiver from the author of the smuggling trick, Hortigosa, to its beneficiary, Lorenza. The subtle trick is so ingenious that it automatically suspends the convention of dramatic irony which places the audience of an *entremés* in a privileged position in relation to the dupe. Lorenza's behaviour once the lover has been smuggled in would puzzle an audience until it achieved its ends. Having entered the room where the lover is hiding, she loudly proclaims her delight in him and her distaste for Cañizares, though she slyly assures the dismayed Cristina, in a remark that also assures the audience, that she is acting to a rational plan ('estoy...en todo mi juicio' [p. 8]). The theatrical secret is that Lorenza's way of deceiving her husband is a novel example of the double-bluffing that was known as *engañando con la verdad*.[37] By getting her lover out of the house without her husband seeing him when the husband purposes to intervene, and then showing her husband an empty room where a lover had seemed to be hidden, she is able to pretend that all she has done is to torment and discredit his jealousy.[38] She strengthens her disguise as a practical joker and adds plausibility to her apparent intention of taunting her husband's jealousy by feigning to disbelieve his claim, which is clearly genuine, that he knew all along that Lorenza was only joking. The temporary effect of mystification firmly makes the *burladora* the more interesting character in the comic climax and makes her trickery all the more impressive, for the audience itself is outwitted. At the same time it extends the drama's comic range by introducing an amusing puzzle that resolves itself as a manifestation of original wit (*agudeza*) on Cervantes' part in its classic form of associating things of dissimilar or opposing kinds. The novelty is that the wit is not verbal but embedded in the situation. Jest is literally paired with earnest: what Lorenza represents as a joke is not in fact a joke; and *engaño* is paired with *verdad*: she literally 'deceives with the truth'.

The *burla* stage of the *entremés* is brought to a close when the couple's shouting attracts the attention of outsiders: an *alguacil* (constable) and some nosy musicians who have been at a nearby wedding. The appearance of these new characters is the prelude to a subtle version of a familiar kind of ending. The *Alguacil* is an authority figure who often appears towards the ends of *entremeses* for the purpose of restoring order when altercations have broken out, and the Musicians' arrival with a *bailarín* amongst their number fore-shadows a normal sequel. By Cervantes' time *entremeses* often closed with a musical rite of *alegría* comprising singing and dancing (in the vigorous style that was known as *baile*, to distinguish it from *danza*, which was physically more restrained). The most notable aspect of the Cervantine version of this musical custom is the use of dramatic irony. The Musicians are outsiders: they do not know what has happened. The song they sing in celebration of the return of matrimonial harmony thus enriches the *engaño* theme and in dramatic terms is a droll celebration of Lorenza's successful *burla*.[39]

El viejo celoso is a lighthearted work but is not a vacuous one. Whilst conserving the levity that was conventionally required of *entremeses*, it brings to the genre the morally useful 'exemplarity' that Cervantes claimed for his pioneering *Novelas*. Even the *burla* has a contribution to make to this edifying aspect of the play.

Had it taken a less surprising form, Lorenza's trickery would have been just funny, given that trickery was a typical source of humour in *entremeses*. The lesson that its originality empowers it to teach warns its public to be wary of preconceptions. The *burla* shows that certain people are 'different' and that any preconception of someone that is based on norms is bound to be fallible. In a certain sense that flatters Cervantes, the message is the medium. The *ejemplo* is one that transcends the technique of direct illustration, or 'mirroring' life as it was often called, and makes the author/public relation-ship an instrument of exemplarity. Behind the daring and clever wife, who is an exceptional figure by real-life standards in husband-deception and by dramatic standards in comic trickery, is the 'different' *entremesista*: the Cervantes who achieves a high and unconventional level of originality as a comic dramatist.

The *burla* makes the general theme of *El viejo celoso* the surprise that awaits people who do not fully know themselves or another person with whom they have formed a relationship. It underscores the human perspective from which Cervantes looks at marriage. The general matrimonial lesson is that men and women ought not to marry unless they are sure that they know themselves, know each other, and are sure that they are natural partners. Its particular purpose is to proclaim the natural needs of young women, the different needs of very old husbands, and the evils of jealousy, viewed as the natural and dominant passion of an old man who has taken a young wife.

On the 'mirror' level of exemplarity the *entremés* is an illustration of wisdom condensed in proverbs. The theme of mutual disenchantment is reminiscent of 'No conforma con el viejo la moza' (Correas, p. 257a) whilst the jealousy theme transmits the wisdom of 'Marido celoso nunca tiene reposo' (ibid., p. 526a) and 'Hombre celoso de suyo se es cornudo' (ibid., p. 169a) and other proverbs like it, the sense of which is that a jealous man brings cuckoldry upon himself. The jealousy theme is an ironical one that depicts a vicious circle. The husband's awareness of his own deficiencies makes him jealous, and his jealousy inclines him to lock up his wife in the home. The sexually frustrated wife resents her imprisonment more intensely than she would if she were sexually content, and it merely exacerbates her frustration. It shows how sexual appetite is sharpened by social confinement, an idea that in the novella is aired in the words of the popular song, 'Madre, la mi madre,/guardas me ponéis' (pp. 37-8). Cañizares' distrustfulness is therefore counter-productive. It makes Lorenza more conscious of her sexual deprivation, causes her to despise her husband, and disposes her to take a lover when she is given the opportunity to do so. Her novel *burla* is in part her way of taking revenge on Cañizares for behaving so oppressively.

Unlike the novella, the *entremés* is not an example of how difficult it is to 'guard' a woman's chastity. The circumstances which provide the wife in *El celoso extremeño* with the opportunity to cuckold her husband possess a very a high degree of causal probability, but the circumstances in the *entremés* appear fortuitous and are not even fully explained. Hortigosa calls at Lorenza's house for unknown reasons when her husband for the first time ever has forgotten to lock the door, and she happens to be the ideal person for arranging the wife's liberation. This difference is important. In *El celoso extremeño* Cervantes is less intent on cautioning people about *matrimonio desigual* than mocking the complacency of husbands in the wealthy aristocratic class whose marriages are shallow. In *El viejo celoso* he is simply intent on cautioning old unmarried men, together with young unmarried women and the latter's parents and guardians, about age-unequal marriage.

He achieves these ends more effectively in the *entremés* than he does in the novella. The partners in the *entremés* are more 'typical' in their respective roles of *viejo* and *moza* and disenchantment is a stronger motif. The husband's jealousy owes nothing to a special character-flaw; it is purely and simply a satirical version of that of a married old man. Furthermore he does not need to be cuckolded, or to think that he has been cuckolded, in order to regret having married, unlike Carrizales in the novella. A similar difference exists between the two wives. Lorenza in the *entremés* does not need to be sexually tempted in order to become frustrated, for she knows what she is missing. Leonora, in contrast, is sexually dormant until Loaysa bursts in on the scene, and her adulterous desires are not necessarily fully self-conscious until her *dueña* incites her to commit the sin. Lorenza, moreover, provides the more direct warning against marrying an old man for money. She herself was seduced by the economic argument and she shows it falling flat. The prospect of a rich inheritance pales into insignificance in Lorenza's mind beside her sexual and social frustration, and her social confinement ruins her taste for expensive clothes and jewellery, the typical gifts of a rich husband with which Cañizares naïvely attempts to ingratiate himself and to deaden her sexual sensibilities.

What the *entremesista* cannot do is to produce a work that is morally and emotionally pungent. One consequence of this is that the *viejo* husband is depicted in a satirical style that tends towards the absurd. He is sexually impotent, ruptured, distressed by a bladder complaint, and presented therefore as a more senile man than his counterpart in the novella. Whilst Carrizales displays an elderly man's intolerance of mental stress, eventually suffering a heart-attack when he is given a severe shock, he is neither completely impotent nor specifically attributed with undignified ill health; he is merely said to have 'muchas indisposiciones' that make him a light sleeper (p. 37). On the other hand, though Cañizares is not a man with an inborn pathological problem, his jealousy is no less grotesque than that of Carrizales. In one respect it is in fact more extreme. As she reveals at the very beginning of the play, Lorenza has spent her entire matrimonial life cooped up inside the home. Leonora, however, is given the minimum social freedom that she realistically needs to be given: she is allowed to go to church, despite the fact that her husband is the 'most jealous man in the world'. Note too how the husband in the *entremés* is stripped of lifelike pride. *Honor* presides over Cañizares' first conversation with his wife, but it is made to speak absurdly. He cautions his wife about saying defamatory things about him in conversations she holds with herself: 'No querría que tuviésedes algún soliloquio con vos misma que redundase en mi perjuicio' (p. 6).[40]

Another form of levity in the *entremés* is merry play with names, which is a typical source of humour in this genre. The name *Cañizares*, which is comparable to the English surname *Reedes*, is an authentic but very unusual one and is whimsical when paired with the surname *Hortigosa*. The latter is another authentic name but again is a rare one alluding to vegetation. The juxtapositioning of the two names naturally makes their rarity and their associations with vegetation amusing. The funnier name is *Hortigosa*, for its vegetable connections are instantly brought out by its owner's gender and the termination *-osa*. Used as the name of a female character, it acquires an adjectival sense equivalent to *Nettlesome* (Honig's translation of the name). It may be a characternym (a name that describes a character) that alludes to Hortigosa's vexatious effect on Cañizares as his interfering *vecina*.[41]

The major limitations of the *entremés* as a work that cultivates levity are that it cannot deal with male *honor* in a plausible way and cannot set its action amongst the nobility. There are two signs that Cañizares is not a member of the nobility. Dramatic convention required the use of a first name preceded by *don* to indicate *hidalguía*, and this style is never used in references to Cañizares. Another sign is the common class of his wife, though this is somewhat less suggestive, given that he did not marry in order to generate heirs. The unfaithful wife is strongly etched as a woman of common class. Her informal speech, her incomprehension of linguistic pomposity coming from her husband (p. 6) and her impatience with such diction, the signs of a superstitious mind, her cheekiness, and the name Lorenza, which is less refined than Leonora, are all indications that she comes from a common background. Her libidinous niece is evidently her blood relation. She can hardly be the *sobrina carnal* of the ancient Carrizales, and she too is implicitly common. She talks in much the same way as her aunt, and her references to nurse-like duties performed for her uncle evoke a female social type from the poorer common class: an unwanted girl who has been taken in by a married relation and who earns her keep by helping in the relative's house.[42] Hortigosa is also common. The service she performs for the frustrated wife and the panache with which she renders it are obvious signs that she is a clandestine *alcahueta*: a procuress, though probably not a *madame*.

In *El viejo celoso* Cervantes achieves artistic novelty in a confining genre and succeeds in making a 'humble' drama a more intelligent and significant one than routinely was the case. A traditional comic mechanism is memorably reinvented, the simple is combined with the subtle, and the *entremés* is evidently *ejemplar*; Cervantes would have claimed, no doubt, that it blended *burlas* with *veras*, using these terms in their contemporary antithetical senses of frivolities, or comic fantasies, and truths or realities.

All this reflects authorial ambitions that are also personal tastes. At the point at which Cervantes asserts a distinctive authorial identity within the work by departing from *entremés* convention, he identifies himself with its three superior qualities: novelty, subtlety and significance. These are qualities that we rediscover in more complex forms in the corresponding novella.

Novela del celoso extremeño

The *ocho entremeses* made no contribution to the general development of Spanish comic drama, as far as we can see. The *Novelas ejemplares*, on the other hand, were a momentous contribution to the development of fiction. With this volume Cervantes established the Spanish offspring of the novella collections of Italy. He also set new standards within the tradition. He raised the novella's moral tone (though he did not rid it of authorial malice, as *El celoso extremeño* shows), he increased its human and moral depth and technical sophistication, and he gave it greater suppleness and versatility, partly by importing techniques and tastes that had gained his approval from the contemporary Spanish theatre. In Cervantes' hands the novella becomes the contemporary equivalent of the elusive 'modern novel'. Its main limitations are its length,[43] its subordination to a neo-Aristotelian doctrine of representation that anchors fiction in the real world and normally requires it to be verisimilar (see n. 6), and its formal propriety in dealing with sex, which is scrupulous both by present-day standards and the typical standards of the Italian *novellieri*.

El celoso extremeño is one of Cervantes' more supple novellas and one of the more dramatic. It can be envisaged as a work in four unequal chapters, so to speak: two whose form is entirely narrative, apart from a brief interior monologue in which Carrizales ponders marriage (p. 21) that is contained in the first of them; one long and highly dramatic chapter in a comic key; and one shorter chapter that is dramatic in a tragic key. The tone shift between the third and final chapters is reminiscent of the hybridity of many *comedias*, though it is unusual by dramatic standards in representing a linear shift in a tragic direction rather than an integration of the Classical dramatic styles (solemn action interspersed with comic action) with a denouement contrived in the happy tradition of comedy.

The first chapter rapidly deals with the hero's life from the time of his youth as far as the time when he conceives his wish for heirs, a period of about forty-eight years (pp. 19-20). The second chapter, covering only a year or so, increases the weight of detailed episode and completes preparations for the matrimonial plot. It first introduces Leonora; it then deals with Carrizales' approach to her parents, their vetting of each other's credentials, the wedding and the attack of *celos*, and at greater length with the husband's domestic security measures, the beginning of the couple's life together, and the marriage's brief success (pp. 20-4). It draws to a close with two rapid allusions to the futility of the security measures and to the novella's tragic end. The second of these predicts the misunderstanding:

No se vio monasterio tan cerrado, ni monjas más recogidas, ni manzanas de oro tan guardadas. Y con todo esto no pudo [Carrizales] en ninguna manera prevenir ni excusar de caer en lo que recelaba; a lo menos, en pensar que había caído. (p. 24)

The remaining chapters cover periods of days. The third and longest deals with Loaysa's appearance on the scene and his progress towards his sexual goal as far as the point at which Marialonso agrees to act as his procuress (pp. 24-40). It is rich in dialogue, strong in its appeal to the reader's sensuous imagination, and reminiscent of *entremeses* both in its comic mechanisms and in its introduction of popular song and dance. Being relevant to the novella's themes, the lyrical material is also reminiscent of *comedias*, where songs attuned to the subject-matter were often introduced in the body of the work. Its main component is the popular song whose refrain is a version of the proverbial truth that a woman is hard to 'guard':

> Madre, la mi madre,
> guardas me ponéis,
> *que si yo no me guardo,*
> *no me guardaréis.* (p. 37)

The final chapter deals with Marialonso's success in acting as the procuress, with the sexual encounter itself, and with the misunderstanding that culminates in Carrizales' death, Leonora's retirement to the convent and Loaysa's flight to the colonies (pp. 40-5). It reaches its climax in the long and riveting monologue that Carrizales speaks to his parents-in-law in the presence of Marialonso and Leonora, who faints on hearing her husband's accusation.

In ending the novella Cervantes makes a formal statement about what it signifies as a *novela ejemplar*, his basic observation repeating the lesson of the refrain in the popular song. The novella shows 'lo poco que hay que fiar de llaves, tornos y paredes cuando queda la voluntad libre' (p. 45).

Whilst the dramatic chapters possess a clear organic unity of the intrigue-based kind to be found in most *comedias*, the novella's overall continuity is grounded in the theme of *engaño* and its supple but intrinsic exemplarity. Though this quality is not fully apparent, and perhaps is one whose innermost facets Cervantes himself did not fully discern until he re-read and revised the text, exemplarity is the mainspring of this work.

El celoso extremeño is a more ample, profound and personal treatment of the theme of *engaño* than the corresponding *entremés*. It is less confined by the subject of irresponsible marriage; it attacks naïvety on a wider front; its parameters are philosophical and theological rather than purely practical, social and secular; and it is more individual. On the deepest level of exemplarity it considers the human condition. On this level it is a Christian reflection on the nature and limits of human freedom in relation to the external world and the self. Cervantes attacks complacency – purposes, habits of mind, and doctrinaire beliefs that exceed the limits that God has placed on security and rational certainty.

The novella's basic moral lesson is that a husband who tries to safeguard his wife against sexual temptation is trying to achieve the impossible. The explanation that is explicitly given is that one person cannot imprison another person's will, but this is the tip of an intellectual iceberg. The deeper explanation is that it cannot be possible to deprive a person of responsibility in a fallen world where all are under divine judgement and must acquire individual guilt or merit. The traditional Roman Catholic belief that mortal life is a moral trial is a basic formative influence on the tale, as we shall see at a later point. This deeper explanation itself forms part of a general view of the relative power of nature and human artifice. The novella implies that when artifice controls nature (all forces in the created world that are not of man's own making), it is only because God allows it to and is not because artificial power is inherently greater than nature. The control that is gained is always insecure. Cervantes introduces this idea in his account of Carrizales' voyage to the Indies, when he deftly refers to the good fortune of sailors whom the elements permit to reach their destinations: 'el cual viaje fue tan próspero que, sin recibir algún revés ni contraste, llegaron al puerto de Cartagena' (p. 19). Behind this allusion to the riskiness of navigation there lies the idea that it is dangerous to exceed the limits which nature has set on human activity. Such thinking was typical of contemporary writers who were haunted by the sense that the advance of materialist civilisation was, in fact, detrimental to human health and happiness, and who were deeply disillusioned with the worlds in which they themselves lived. The example is also conventional. Maritime travel was notoriously perilous, and ships were a favourite emblem of the dangerous use of artifice to subvert the natural order.[44]

In one respect the novella is deeply polemical. It is important to distinguish individual freedom as Cervantes depicts it from the theological concept of free will (*libre albedrío*) as the Catholic Church understood it. This was the idea that despite the fact that Original Sin (Adam's sin) has corrupted human nature, all human beings possess the power to reject evil and to will themselves into a harmonious relationship with God, a relationship in which they are further perfected by His supernatural grace. The novella's ending has been seen as an affirmation of free will in the theological sense, or something closely resembling it. But this view needs to be challenged. Whilst Cervantes' picture of human freedom is in other respects a conventional one, it does not present a conventional view of choice. *El celoso extremeño* prefers an essentially social conception of the freedom of the human will to the moral conception expounded by Catholic theologians. On the one hand it stresses that the human will is autonomous in a social sense. Human beings do what they want to do in any social situation in which they are faced with choice: they cannot be forced to conform to laws, conventions, norms, or expectations, if they do not wish to conform. Furthermore they cannot be imprisoned in any condition which denies them the power of moral self-definition – the power to assert themselves in the defining sense of displaying qualities which give them a moral identity as individuals. On the other hand the novella very strongly suggests that all behaviour is the outcome of disposition: that it is a manifestation of a person's basic typology (e.g. male, female, young, or old) and of the nuanced disposition, something like our idea of 'character', that Cervantes refers to as a person's *condición* (e.g. Carrizales is *celoso* and *llano*, whilst Leonora is *tierna*, *llana* and *simple*). It is therefore a work whose author favours a determinist view of human choice and not the view that was taken by the Roman Catholic Church. Its major challenge to Catholic theology is a suggestion that places Cervantes' mind in league with the more pessimistic forms of contemporary Protestantism: namely, that spiritual salvation is not available to all people; whether by birth, by social training, or under the combined effect of the two, there are some whose adult dispositions are pathologically sinful. This suggestion is most strongly made through the fictional example of a complete life that is protagonised by Carrizales, who in some degree stands for the wealthier ranks of the Spanish nobility.

The religious censors who examined books may not have regarded the novella's determinist inclinations as dangerous enough to warrant attention or they may simply not have grasped them. As shallow readers when dealing with non-doctrinal works, they probably did not grasp them.[45] Though the word *voluntad* occurs no less than fifteen times in Cervantes' text, *libertad* is a word that occurs but once – in the social context of freeing slaves (p. 45) – and no mention is made of *libre albedrío*. The novella, therefore, is not concerned explicitly with free will. Furthermore its problematisation of Catholic theology does not lie in the behavioural facts as Cervantes verbally records them, but in their possible or probable significance for a reader of independent judgement who shrewdly looks behind them. The varying style and chronologically unbalanced way in which Cervantes constructs the fictional life of Carrizales further obscure the theological issue by obscuring his deep consistency. His moral identity is built up, triptych-like, in three chapters of different kinds with the second and third being separated in narrative time: the account of his life until he first sees Leonora (fictional biography); the beginning of the marriage; and its catastrophic end.

The exemplarity of *El celoso extremeño* is consistent with the hint which Cervantes heavily drops in the Prologue that the *Novelas* require an inquisitive and able readership. It transcends the 'facts' as Cervantes records them and their significance as he states it, reaches beyond traditional wisdom, and entails the use of innovative methods to teach unusual lessons. All in all *El celoso extremeño* is perhaps the novella that most justifies the Prologue-writer who promises *sabroso fruto*, but who effectively offers it only to those who read well enough – 'look' well enough, in Cervantes' vocabulary – to find it without his help.[46]

Especially in its final form, it is both original and elitist. It seeks to establish a special rapport with a superior public that Cervantes would have called *discreto*: 'discerning'.[47] This public is made up of adaptable and shrewd readers who have relatively independent minds but who share the author's personal interests and sensibilities and who therefore bring an appropiately biassed mentality to bear upon the text. The beginning of this special relationship may well be Cervantes' light-handed allusion to the moral-philosophical *topos* of the arrogance of shipping, which serves to introduce the theme of the sovereign power of nature. It reaches its climax in the puzzled comment that Cervantes passes at the novella's end on the behaviour of the maligned wife. In his final sentence Cervantes claims to be mystified by what he apparently takes to have been her absurdly pusillanimous attitude towards her husband's delusion:

Sólo no sé qué fue la causa que Leonora no puso más ahínco en disculparse y dar a entender a su celoso marido cuán limpia y sin ofensa había quedado en aquel suceso; pero la turbación le ató la lengua, y la prisa que se dio a morir su marido no dio lugar a su disculpa.   (p. 45)

Outwardly a form of authorial self-criticism for a reader who feels that the heroine's behaviour is indeed inexplicable, or evidence of the author's obtuseness about the character, or, at best, a genial invitation to 'see if you can make sense of her', the concluding remark is really an ironical one that supplements the preceding statement about what the novella signifies as an 'ejemplo y espejo'. The preceding statement is a very elementary account of the fiction's exemplarity. It is a formulation of 'mirror' meaning that uses plain and concrete language, reflects the emphasis of earlier comment, and is presumably addressed to an idea of an average reader. The final statement is another version of the tale's significance that transcends both the style and range of the public version and communicates with the superior reader whom Cervantes would have called *discreto*.

The novella's stated or public message is in essence an individualised version of the folk wisdom according to which a woman is very hard to 'guard', or it is pointless to try to 'guard' a woman who wishes to be free. It refers to the failure of Carrizales' security measures and comprises two ideas, both of which attack the hero's naïvety. Behind them there lie the related themes of the sovereign power of nature, the inevitability of temptation in a world that is under judgement, and the individual's social autonomy. The first idea is that a husband who locks his wife away does not in fact secure her chastity because no one can shackle another person's will. The second idea is that a wife's virtue is especially unsafe if she is young and inexperienced and looked after by a *dueña*. Cervantes finally images *dueñas* as hypocritical nuns, through descriptive reference to their nun-like uniforms:

Y yo quedé con el deseo de llegar al fin de este suceso, ejemplo y espejo de lo poco que hay que fiar de llaves, tornos y paredes cuando queda la voluntad libre; y de lo menos que hay que confiar de verdes y pocos años, si les andan al oído exhortaciones destas dueñas de monjil negro y tendido y tocas blancas y luengas.   (p. 45)

The stated lesson emerges from the collapse of a marriage that in certain repects is more abnormal than its counterpart in the *entremés*. The wife is younger and is so ignorant about the opposite sex, her own nature and marriage customs that she finds no fault in her spouse. Whereas Lorenza is knowledgeable enough to despise Cañizares for his jealousy, Leonora even falls in love with her husband in a childishly platonic way.[48] Her feelings for him help to make the unnatural marriage an exceptionally successful one in its early days and correspondingly to make its undoing especially impressive as a cautionary 'example'. It particularly shows that not even a wife who loves her husband is immune to temptation if her love is merely affectionate and not erotic.

Leonora would have remained in her infantile state had it not been for Loaysa's intervention. Loaysa is the channel through which temptation enters her life in accordance with the laws of nature and the purposes of God. Both Loaysa's arrival on the scene and his steady progress towards his goal are therefore endowed with a high degree of causal probability. His intervention is well explained by his idleness, moral condition, and the support he gets from his degenerate friends, and by Carrizales' inability to marry and live with Leonora in social secrecy. Carrizales would have needed a priest and witnesses in order to get married; banns must have been published; he has parents-in-law; he needs someone to supply the house with provisions; and on holy days he must take his wife to Mass, to satisfy her expectations and the requirements of the Church; the only precaution he is able to take is to go to church at an unsociably early hour. To make matters worse for him, his house exudes an air of mystery that inevitably attracts enquiry. Word was bound to get around and sooner or later to find the knave who would storm Carrizales' fortress.

Whilst the knave is introduced in a thoroughly realistic way, the intrigue that he then leads continues the theme of nature outwitting artifice in a comic style that laughs at gullibility. Leonora is a caricature of a naïve wife, whilst the servants are caricaturesque examples of naïve disloyalty which are probably intended to mock the social ignorance of rich and aristocratic husbands who trust their domestic staff. The comic style owes much to the humour of the *entremés* tradition. Loaysa, who is a satirist's hero in this part of the tale, is himself related to the *burladores* of *entremeses* in each of their traditional guises: those of trickster and joker. He does not merely deceive his victims but also indulges a taste for privately mocking them. They themselves are reminiscent of the earliest and most dependable type of comic dupe in the *entremés* tradition: the *bobo* (idiot), who was a character inherited from *pasos*.[49] In one way or another, Loaysa's victims all display a risible vulnerability that invests his progress towards his goal with a satirical form of the deterministic verisimilitude of his first appearance on the scene. The whole intrigue contributes in a cynically amusing style to the first part of the novella's public message. At the same time it smugly tightens up the meaning of the ominous statement that Cervantes had made before introducing Loaysa into the tale: 'no pudo [Carrizales] en ninguna manera prevenir ni excusar de caer en lo que recelaba; a lo menos, en pensar que había caído' (p. 24). The words 'no pudo en ninguna manera' harbour the fatalistic sense: 'inevitably couldn't'.

Cervantes here is not alluding simply to the hero's inability to protect himself against cuckoldry. He is also suggesting that Carrizales could not have prevented his jealousy from making his sudden disillusionment the source of another delusion (the belief that his wife was an adulteress), though the fatalistic implication of this aspect of the statement lies less close to the surface. The qualifying clause 'en pensar que había caído' is detached from the words 'no pudo en ninguna manera prevenir ni excusar', with the result that its only meaning may appear to be that the hero's fears will not be fulfilled in the way in which we spontaneously think of fears being fulfilled (the feared thing actually happens and is not merely believed to have happened). Nevertheless Cervantes' statement contains a fatalistic reading not only of the destruction of the security measures, but also of the destruction of Leonora's virtue in the eyes of Carrizales. In this respect it alludes to the tragic irony that the husband who sought to lock out sin was probably sin's own prisoner.

In the final chapter the clockwork world of *burlador* and *bobo* disappears from between the lines of Cervantes' text as the fiction becomes a christian-ised and more complex version of the most powerful type of Classical tragedy. This was a type of tragic drama whose hero fell, as Aristotle put it, through his own 'error' or 'failure' (*hamartia*), but who appeared to be fore-doomed. Though the hero made his own decisions, his fall was 'probable' or 'necessary'[50] and it usually reflected the will of some divine power or a supernatural Fate. In Cervantes' adaptation of this Classical genre, the tragic hero is Carrizales, 'failure' is sin, and 'probability' or 'necessity' is rooted in disposition. God and the Devil are the presiding supernatural powers.

The event that precipitates the tragic ending is Carrizales' early recovery from the effects of the ointment that his wife had used to put him to sleep whilst she, Loaysa, and her imprisoned companions held their private party. It is this event that exposes the husband to the nightmare that his security measures have hitherto kept in check. We are told that God 'decreed' it: 'Y en esto ordenó el cielo que a pesar del ungüento, Carrizales despertase' (p. 41). The modern reader may find this remark a puzzling one, given that in an earlier statement Cervantes referred to the Devil ('el sagaz perturbador del género humano' [p. 23]) as the supernatural cause of trouble in Carrizales' marriage; but the two statements are, in fact, complementary. The earlier statement embodies a Christian perspective on events that is subsumed in the more complex significance of the later statement in which God is given a role. The full implications of the second statement are that Carrizales' error is born of sin, is triggered by temptation and is willed by the Devil, but occurs because God, who is both omniscient and omnipotent, purposely allows it to occur. The essential theological view at work in the statement is that God puts man on trial. God has so ordered human life that it infallibly produces trials of goodness, the results of which are consequential in this world and the next, where they decide the eternal destiny of the soul. To put the first part of this idea in another way, God has allowed the Devil a role in every-body's life, to ensure that they are tempted. Complementing these beliefs in their 'correct' theological form was the doctrine of free will. It stood to reason that if human beings were under judgement, and if God, their judge, was perfectly good, they must have moral freedom. If they did not, God could not be just. In traditional thinking, God could be said to decree wrongdoing only in the sense that He possessed 'foreknowledge' of how people would behave, and 'permitted' them to do wrong.[51]

Cervantes' novella shows faint support for the doctrine of *libre albedrío* but is pervaded by the complementary belief that life is a trial of goodness. All the major turning-points are moral trials for characters. Carrizales is the most tested character and he is the one who produces the most sinister results. The marriage itself is the result of a trial that mainly tests the hero. Carrizales not only failed the test but in typical fashion he approached it in a self-reliant way and did not understand the issues. Having decided in principle to marry Leonora on the strength of his own self-centred reasoning, he presumed that God had guided him to her because He desired the marriage: 'Alto, pues; echada está la suerte, y ésta es la que el cielo quiere que yo tenga' (p. 21). Turning to God in an afterthought that reinforces a decision he has made already, he confuses God with the Devil, for it must be Satan who wills the marriage of a very young woman and an elderly man with an acutely jealous nature. His early recovery from the effects of the ointment belongs to a series of three moral tests that he undergoes as a married man, in each of which he maintains his record of failure. This series of matrimonial tests helps to show that people must carry responsibility for their moral mistakes and that in any given situation failure will lead to further testing in which more is put at risk. The first trial after the wedding is the instant attack of jealousy, the hero's strongest passion. This tests his will to mortify the special weakness that ought to have made him a celibate man throughout his life, but which he had conveniently thought would not be triggered by marriage with a mere girl. The way in which he responds to the trial is the opposite of what he ought to have done and merely ensures that his wife's temptation occurs in artificial conditions that intensify the power of evil, disadvantaging her and working against her husband's interests as a man intent on forestalling cuckoldry. The next test is the shocking scene that he witnesses in the *dueña*'s room after God has 'decreed' his early awakening: his wife in bed, asleep in the arms of a stranger. This second matrimonial test is the equivalent in Carrizales' life of the destruction of his security measures in the life of Leonora. The latter event was inevitable, theologically, precisely because it exposed Leonora to temptation, thwarting her husband's virtual wish to interfere with the natural and divine order of life. The early awakening is a similar sort of event. Carrizales' will to mortify his jealousy is now tested in a way that forces the moral issue. Denying him access to further protection against his jealous fears, it compels him to choose between trusting his wife or convicting her of the sexual crime of which his jealousy wishes to convict her.

He cannot possibly pass this test unless he first sees that the evidence is inconclusive. He must then calmly question his wife, showing neither anger nor the inclination to despair. By speaking to her in this way he would nurture her trust and hope in him and, in so doing, would encourage her to give a detailed and trustworthy account of what had happened, if the appearances of great guilt were in fact deceptive. To do what is required of him, he needs the virtues that eluded him when he decided to get married, and again when, his jealous nature having rebelled, he locked his wife up in the home. The requisite virtues are the four 'cardinal virtues' of Christianity: the moral virtues of temperance, fortitude and justice, and the intellectual virtue of prudence. Carrizales' consistent weakness is that he lacks the will to exercise these virtues. The root cause is the sinful state of his soul. On all the occasions when the hero is tested, he needs to show a magnanimity that he can only achieve by supernatural grace; that is to say, through the gifts of faith and hope, which would help, in part, by fixing his higher desires in God and not in worldly things (his relationship with God would matter more to him than Leonora's fidelity), and through charitable love. These were the three 'theological virtues' all of which were divine gifts accessible only to people who were spiritually disposed to receive them. Had Carrizales possessed these virtues, his will would have inclined in the right direction and his *llano* or 'straightforward' mentality would have accelerated the correct decision. However, inasmuch as his inclinations are rooted in his selfish passions, he is not in a position to receive the virtues he needs, and his *llano* mentality reinforces his corrupt will: he believes and does what a sinful and straightforward mind naturally sees as the obvious truth and obvious thing to do. A Catholic theologian might confidently have accused him of stubbornness. A discerning layman would surely have entertained the idea that he failed his tests inevitably, through a predestination that might be labelled 'fate'.

The third matrimonial trial tests his will to revise his judgement of his wife. At the same time it forces the spiritual issue, inviting the hero to consider the state of his eternal soul, to recognise the full extent of his errors, and to repent in the Christian way. His distressed condition quickly brings on a heart-attack (the symptoms are clear) which inevitably produces a faint: 'sin ser poderoso a otra cosa, se dejó caer desmayado' (p. 41). From this he recovers in a state of exhaustion and with premonitions of death. Knowing that he is about to die, he is witness to evidence that he may have misjudged his wife. This evidence lies in her behaviour. Probably the more significant evidence is the affection that she shows for him when he tells her that he is dying, and the goodwill, humility and candour she displays when she tries to persuade him that she offended him only 'in thought'. However, the signs that Carrizales himself is guilty of a sin of thought that is much more serious than the kind to which his wife confesses are interpreted by him as hypocrisy. He misreads the signs partly because they are, in fact, ambiguous from his own perspective within the fiction, but mainly because his will is still corrupt. Though no better than could be reasonably expected under the given circumstances, the signs he is given are inadequate to his needs. Although he shows a certain sense of responsibility for what he thinks has taken place and does perform a kind of penance, he has not undergone the deep conversion that would dispose him to reconsider his accusation against his wife. The best that the approach of death produces in Carrizales is an impious kind of self-reversal that is reminiscent of his earthbound and *llano* repentance as another Prodigal Son: 'un otro Pródigo' (p. 19), a phrase in which 'un otro' signals difference. This consisted in reversing himself out of prodigality into industrious wealth-production. Now he turns his jealous possessiveness back-to-front by willing his wife to her lover. True to form, his repentance is governed by mental *llaneza* unperfected by grace.

His big speech, addressed chiefly to his parents-in-law, is the novella's most impressive example of direct characterisation. It is shot through with tension and cant. We should not believe Carrizales' forgiveness of his wife. He knows very well that the responsibility for what he believes has taken place ultimately lies with him, as the author of a marriage which he now concedes was foolish; but he does not, in his heart, exonerate his wife for proving that the marriage was wrong. He still has feelings of tenderness towards her that are inspired by her pretty face, as he reveals, for example, when he refers to her as a 'gem' (*joya*); but morally he despises her. He spittingly calls her 'ésta', not 'Leonora', at the point at which he discloses how he found her. Furthermore his self-pity and pride colour his view of the past, making his recollection of it a kind of sophistry. He virtually claims that the way in which he treated his wife could not have been more caring and responsible, and that her infidelity was ungrateful and unjust. His exculpation of Leonora is presumably a way of dignifying himself in his own, her, and her parents' eyes and partly a reflection of the anger he feels towards himself for deciding to marry her.

The anger he feels towards himself, and probably his sense of what the occasion demands of him, underlie his display of piety. He rebukes himself in the name of a God who punishes those who do not place all their desires and hopes in Him; in other words, a God who punished Carrizales for placing his desires in Leonora and hopes in domestic security:

> Mas como no se puede prevenir con diligencia humana el castigo que la voluntad divina quiere dar a los que en ella no ponen del todo en todo sus deseos y esperanzas, no es mucho que yo quede defraudado en las mías; y que yo mismo haya sido el fabricador del veneno que me va quitando la vida. (p. 43)

The idea that God has willed an adultery is as implausible as Carrizales' suggestion later on in his speech that the arrangement of an adulterer's marriage can be counted as an *obra pía*. This God is really an extension of Carrizales' own nature. He equates adultery with cuckoldry, and therefore sees it as a suitable way of punishing someone for their infidelity to Him. God, in fact, punished Carrizales by allowing him to punish himself, i.e. by letting him be deceived by the Devil.

Carrizales' Christian thought is shallow, corrupt and deluded. It is also a red herring, for he is not seeking God's forgiveness any more than he is genuinely forgiving his wife. In part he is coming to terms with his own conscience as a proud man who must deal with his guilt entirely on his own. He is expiating the anger he bears towards himself by the *llano* means of reversing the basic mistake he made in marrying Leonora. He is lashing out at his past. Hence he calls his plan a *venganza* that he is inflicting upon himself. He is also coping with humiliation and bitterness by seeing and representing himself as a responsible and loving husband who is magnanimous in death. At the same time he is coping with death by courting posthumous fame. He is plotting to become a unique example in the outside world of altruism on the part of a dying husband, though he is less hopeful of being remembered for *bondad* (goodness) than for extraordinary *simplicidad*, perhaps because his dispositions for his widow's future security could seem harsh to a world that was unaware that she was marrying her lover, or perhaps because in choosing Loaysa to fill his place he might be deemed to have shown poor judgement of character:

> Mas por que todo el mundo vea el valor de los quilates de la voluntad y fe con te quise, en este último trance de mi vida quiero mostrarlo de modo que quede en el mundo por ejemplo, si no de bondad, al menos de simplicidad jamás oída ni vista. (p. 44)

Note how the phrase *mostrar el valor* invites the reader to compare Carrizales with the wife whose *valor* was such that she resisted the crime of which she has been convicted ('el valor de Leonora fue tal que...lo mostró contra las fuerzas de su astuto engañador' [p. 41]). Leonora achieves a real victory against the moral evil that besets her, but no such victory is won by Carrizales. He fails to see that his marriage was selfish; he does not repent of his jealousy; and he conquers his jealousy only in the sense that he is generous in death. Furthermore his generosity is impious, for he plots a sacrilegious marriage which would unite a pair of adulterers; and his basic motives are bitterness, anger and pride; not love for his wife, justice, or moral humility.

His failure to redeem himself is his own responsibility from a theological point of view, but from the same point of view God foresaw and allowed it, and from an empirical viewpoint it is 'necessary', as Aristotle would have put it. This impression is reinforced when his failure is seen in the broader context of his life. Though Cervantes gives only a thumbnail sketch of him as he was in his bachelor years, the complete picture strongly suggests that he was someone whose adult *condición* held no vocation for spiritual reunion with God: that his life was simply the working out of the Devil's will, which was virtually that of a supernatural Fate.

Carrizales' sense of reality was always that of a self-reliant and self-centred materialist. His Christian faith bore no resemblance to the authentic faith that depends on intuitive knowledge of God and which trustingly seeks His will above all else. It was practically almost meaningless. His sense of danger was earthbound, his goods were worldly, and even by worldly standards they were shallow: pleasure-seeking up to the age of forty-eight, when his money ran out; wealth-creation from forty-eight to sixty-eight;[52] and then comfortable retirement, married to a pretty girl who he hoped would bear him heirs. Although he was not a cruel man in any normal sense of the word, and he had learnt to be *liberal* from a period spent in the army,[53] he had no affinity with theological love. On returning to Spain as a millionaire he had no desire to relieve the poverty of his native Extremadura, seeing it rather as a threat to his social tranquillity (p. 20), and it was the lack of any charitable instinct that first turned his mind towards marriage: he did not really want a wife; what he wanted was heirs. Neither did he show any genuine charity to his wife's impoverished parents. It did occur to him to shower them with gifts, but as a 'liberal' man in Cervantes' account, not as a 'generous' man, and presumably to achieve the comforting effect that his liberality produced: 'aunque tenían lástima a su hija por la estrecheza en que vivía, la templaban con las muchas dádivas que Carrizales, su liberal yerno, les daba' (p. 23). Women he saw as mere servants of his pleasures and needs and as threats to his peace of mind. His interest in marrying Leonora reflected his desire for children to whom he would leave his fortune, his weakness for a pretty face, and a selfish and complacent view of her immaturity. His greatest passion, his jealousy, clearly owed its peculiar intensity not to love but to an insecurity of pride. Once he knew that his wife had betrayed him, he wanted to take her life; and he would indeed have murdered her, had shock and rage not given him a heart-attack.

His wife may be viewed as an identical kind of character: a creature of disposition. She is not a chronic sinner, of course, and she actually achieves a victory over lust. In this sense she represents an implicit warning against trusting stereotypes – in her case, the young wife or single girl who disobeys moral authority when she experiences sexual temptation. On the other hand she is also a morally conventional character in the sense that she conforms to an expectation of young women of good breeding. She contradicts one kind of preconception in which women in general are cynically viewed as sexually unworthy of trust, but ultimately conforms to another kind that discriminates between them in the light of their social class. The latter perspective normally existed in a different zone of the contemporary Spanish psyche – one that wished to believe in ideals, and which naturally embedded its moral ideal of femininity in its ideal conception of the nobility. The ideal view of noble women is, in fact, the one that prevails in narrative fiction and drama. There well-bred women are seldom unchaste unless they are single and have been reckless enough to surrender their virginity in return for a promise of marriage. In *El celoso extremeño* the two preconceptions are brought into contact, however. In the early version it is the levelling perspective that prevails. The brief confirmation of the heroine's seduction is couched as an understated description of how much she enjoys the experience: 'No estaba ya tan llorosa Isabela en los brazos de Loaisa, a lo que creerse puede' (ed. Avalle-Arce, p. 256): she was not as tearful in the seducer's arms 'as one might believe'. One of the aims of reforming the heroine in the published version was perhaps to reduce the novella's social impertinence – a motive like that which underlies the excision of a lengthy account of the Sevillian *gente de barrio*, Loaysa's class, whom the published text leaves relatively undisturbed, 'por buenos respetos', in the narrator's own words (p. 24). The result, however, is a female character who is neither reassuring nor unlikely. On the one hand she is sufficiently weak and individualised to offer faint comfort to aristocratic husbands. On the other hand her sexual behaviour is no less plausible than that of Isabela, her previous incarnation, partly because it ultimately conforms to the ideal of noble femininity, and partly because her embodiment of this ideal is foreshadowed in the distress she shows as Marialonso leads her to the bedroom, almost having to drag her.[54] We shall see later on that Cervantes uses deceptive language in order to give conflicting signals about his plans for Leonora once she has entered the bedroom. Nevertheless it is unlikely that her moral victory would have seemed at all improbable to a contemporary readership. An intelligent reader might in hindsight have regarded the victory as a moral 'necessity' that was seminally revealed before the event, in behavioural evidence he was foolish not to trust.

The love that Leonora displays for Carrizales when he has suffered the heart-attack, her initially supine acceptance of guilt when he has presented his accusation against her, and her pleading of innocence when she discovers his wish that she marry her lover, all appear to be very probable if we note the relevant facts: the *ternura* that is part of the heroine's character (sentimental tenderness, augmented by sensory tenderness: she is acutely sensitive to visual impressions); the platonic nature of her feelings for her husband, which are not in conflict with her sensual feelings for Loaysa;[55] the fact that she has not a shred of evidence to substantiate her innocence, as she herself observes ('no estáis obligado a creerme ninguna cosa de las que os dijere' [p. 45]); the tragic irony that pleading innocence to a disbeliever makes one a bare-faced liar; and the fact that if she married Loaysa she would be marrying herself to guilt, effectively transforming her venial sin of imagining herself as an adulteress – her 'thought crime', reflecting her natural sexuality – into something far more serious.

Her failure to try harder to vindicate herself in her husband's eyes is well explained by the strength of the evidence that is stacked against her and the opprobrium attached to lying. Together with her love for her stricken husband and her awareness that he has always feared what he thinks has taken place (that he has always distrusted her) and with her reluctance to marry Loaysa, these aspects of her situation explain why her failure was also a disability – why she was, in fact, tongue-tied by emotion. As for her decision to enter a convent, it is a probable sequel to her conquest of lust that signifies her repudiation of a marriage that she would detest; and it is foreshadowed in the significant timing of her truncated plea of innocence, which she makes on learning that she is expected to marry Loaysa. It is also consistent with her personal social history – her enclosure as the wife of Carrizales, her habituation to poverty before she married, and her segregation from young men, both in her marriage and probably in her earlier life. Leonora has been prepared very well for the vows of obedience, poverty and chastity that she will need to take in order to become a nun.

From a worldly viewpoint Leonora is the tragic protagonist of the novella. However, when the characters are viewed from a Christian perspective, the tragic protagonist is Carrizales. Leonora is a positive figure when judged by the higher values of Christianity. She passes all her tests: she honours her father and mother (keeps the fifth Commandment) by accepting Carrizales as her husband; she honours both them and Carrizales in her capacity as a wife; and she directly honours God, by choosing to become a bride of Christ rather than marry Loaysa. The second trial she does not pass to perfection, but she is tested in extreme conditions and she fulfils the essential requirement, for she obeys the seventh Commandment: 'You shall not commit adultery'. Although she shows no signs of faith in the strict theological sense, she clearly possesses a vocation for love, and as a bride of Christ her life will presumably be one of spiritual growth culminating in her salvation. Her tragedy is to be unrecognised for what she is in this world and to carry a burden of suffering she does not deserve. In this sense the widow resembles Christ, her new groom, and her painful experience of worldly marriage should enable her to identify with Him more viscerally than she can ever have done before. Carrizales, on the other hand, is a confirmed failure in life, both from a worldly viewpoint, unless we value hoarded wealth, and from a Christian point of view. Furthermore he may well have been an impotent man in the moral and spiritual spheres. If this is understood by the reader, he plainly deserves more pity than Leonora.

Whether or not he actually gets it is of course another matter, but he can only be the less tragic character for a reader who knows that he himself is lacking in Christian love. Partly for this latter reason, the hero acquires a representative tragic status as the focus for a *discreto* reader's anxiety in rationally asking disturbing questions concerning the human predicament and his own spiritual self. Is there really such a thing as free will, in the theological sense? May the damned be simply unfortunate and the saved be simply the lucky? Why should one person's route to salvation apparently depend on another's route to damnation? Am I myself one of the saved?

Carrizales' example has profound implications of a critical nature for contemporary spirituality. It impugns the intellectual authority of the Church, it diminishes the role of human reason in believing in a perfect God, and it increases the importance of faith, the kind of belief that transcends the power of reason. At the same time it locates faith in an individual and loving relationship with a personal God that is probably of a vocational nature.[56] This does not mean that Cervantes himself is in full possession of the theological virtues. It does make him an ironic observer of the spiritual failure of an officially Christian State. Carrizales' example of a hollow and ineffectual kind of Christian faith is reinforced by secondary characterisation. This casts further doubt on free will in the theological sense, highlights the difference between real and empty Christianity, and emphasises the existence of spiritual poverty in the Spanish world and, by extension, the delusion of a nation that defined itself as *católico* or *cristiano*. Except for the heroine, who does so only immaturely, no one shows the least affinity with the central Christian Commandment: 'Love the Lord your God with all your heart, with all your soul, with all your mind, and with all your strength', or its corollary about loving one's neighbour (*Mark* 12: 30-31; cf. *Luke* 10: 27 and *Matthew* 22: 37-39). Leonora's earthly destiny – the secluded convent – reflects the failure of her fellow Christians and chiefly the native Spanish ones, beginning with her own parents, who approached her marriage as a financial investment, to live up to Christ's commandments. Furthermore it is the only strong symbol of spiritual hope for an individual that Cervantes puts into any of his characters' lives. Its opposite is the broad land that lies across the Ocean. Refuge of *desesperados* who have lost all hope in their lives in Spain, sanctuary of the bankrupt, haven of murderers and card-sharps, lure of loose women, and 'engaño común de muchos y remedio particular de pocos', so the narrator says at the tale's beginning, Spanish America is a symbol of the World, the Flesh and the Devil, and of the individual human will disposed to commit spiritual suicide. The convent/America opposition is not just symbolical, however. The particular convent is a real place where people are close to God, and America is the real place where people are closest to Hell. There are therefore both symbolical reasons and 'real-life' reasons, as Cervantes perceives the Spanish world, for making America the destination of Loaysa at the end of the tale. This is not just a subtle form of moral condemnation. It is a statement about the future. Loaysa, so the ending hints, is a Carrizales in the making: another man who will go to his grave as an unregenerate sinner. The narration of the tale's ending is starkly unemotional. This is not a callous or insensitive style but one that reflects the complex and significant nature of what is described, silently appeals to readers' judgement, and leaves them to draw their conclusions. It is typical of the work. The narrator's presentation of events tends to be sparsely matter-of-fact throughout. Such comment as he makes on the whole is ironic, intensifying the appeal to judgement, and emotionally serene. The only very excited comment is that which foreshadows the novella's stated lesson: Cervantes declaims the corruption of *dueñas* and derides the hero for trying to shelter his wife against temptation (pp. 40-1).

Most other comment is blended into the narrative and is ironically indirect. It uses both simple verbal irony[57] and an original and more subtle technique: that of ironical empathy. The latter first appears in the ambiguous form of the initial description of Marialonso as 'una dueña de mucha prudencia y gravedad' (p. 22). As is later confirmed, this describes her not as she is, but as she wishes to appear to the world and as Carrizales mistakenly sees her. The later instances of ironical empathy are statements that in the original text reported the hero's disillusionment in the aftermath of the 'adultery'. These become in the revised version economical ways of presenting Carrizales' delusion and dryly mocking the strength of his conviction:

Y con todo eso tomara la venganza que aquella gran maldad requería, si se hallara con armas para poder tomarla; y así determinó volver a su aposento a tomar una daga y volver a sacar las manchas de su honra con sangre de sus dos enemigos, y aun con toda aquella de toda la gente de su casa. Con esta determinación honrosa y necesaria...   (p. 41)

Oyó la voz de la dulce enemiga suya el desdichado viejo...   (p. 42)[58]

y abrazándose con su esposo, le hacía las mayores caricias que jamás le había hecho, preguntándole qué era lo que sentía, con tan tiernas y amorosas palabras como si fuera la cosa del mundo que más amaba.
(loc. cit.)

The delusion is evoked in the manner of describing the reality: '*como si fuera la cosa del mundo que más amaba*'.

Lloraba Leonora por verle de aquella suerte, y reíase él con una risa de persona que estaba fuera de sí, considerando la falsedad de sus lágrimas.

(loc. cit.)

derramando los dos muchas lágrimas; ella, con no más ocasión de verlas derramar a su esposo; él, por ver cuán fingidamente ella las derramaba. (p. 43)

Irony is the most subtle aspect of the narrator's style and occurs in four main forms: simple irony, empathetic irony, ironic comparison (e.g. of Carrizales' house to a convent), and the irony of ambivalence. One thing that the use of irony always does is underline the fact that language is not reality and that understanding language is an act of interpretation. The proliferation of non-comparative forms of irony (simple irony, empathetic irony, and particularly ironies of ambivalence) says something of the utmost importance about Cervantes' conception of truth, something that is semi-implicit in his interrogation of free will and which distances him from the authority-based and logic-based discipline of theology: namely, that truth is substance, not concept, idea or abstraction: that to know a truth we must hear it speak for itself; we must look at the reality.

The use of irony makes various contributions to the novella's exemplarity. First, it shows how language means what we construe it to mean, can put up false appearances and can possess unspoken depths. Second, it helps to reveal the problematical relationship between language and perception in a world in which truth is more complicated and less absolute than it is commonly understood to be. Here it is part of an investigation of the dangers attached to preconceptualisation. It helps to reveal the inadequacy of the mental dictionaries that we carry around with us as our means of identifying and ordering things, and the importance of not allowing language, as it is conventionally used, to command our sense of reality.

At the centre of this investigation is the sexual behaviour of the heroine. The plot presents an example of infidelity that escapes the pages of the mental dictionary. On the one hand it does not entail the sexual intercourse that is the essential ingredient in adultery or making a husband *cornudo*, nor does it present a wife who firmly asserts a *wish* to commit adultery. On the other hand Leonora is taken to bed by a man who tries to have sexual intercourse with her, and she may not have resisted all his sexual attentions. Cervantes' account of her display of *valor* is both euphemistic and ambiguous. The 'momento que más le convenía' could have been either the beginning of Loaysa's love-making, as distinct from the moment at which he manoeuvred the heroine onto the bed, or a later moment at which he tried to have sexual intercourse. Cervantes' report clearly raises the possibility that Leonora acquiesced in foreplay.[59] At the same time its ambiguity asserts a will to draw a veil across her behaviour which hints at a further complication. Given that she was not a loose woman but a casualty of inexperience, and given that she finally displayed the *valor* of a conscientious wife in conditions that could not have been more trying, it is impertinent to wonder exactly what took place in the private room. This explains why Cervantes uses the superlative phrase 'cuán limpia y sin ofensa' in the final sentence to describe Leonora's behaviour and how he thinks that she herself should have described it to her husband, despite the uncertainty of detail that surrounds it. What he does in this final sentence is re-write the dictionary of moral behaviour as it needs to be re-written to accommodate a Leonora.

The opposite of this Cervantine expansion of the mental dictionary is his hero's imprisonment in narrowmindedness when he finds Leonora in the bed. In this episode we are shown at least two truths concerning the tricky relationship between appearances or surface meaning as we find it in observed reality (*prima facie* evidence) and cognition. Firstly that appearances and reality can be so different that the truth is done for if the observer has no motivation to question the appearances. Secondly that when evidence consists of a type of thing (in this case, a wife secretly sleeping with a stranger) that is normally part of something else (adultery) from which it is not precisely distinguished in the vocabulary of conceptualisation (there is no word, in Spanish or English, that discriminates between what Leonora committed and the act of adultery), it is bound to be confused with the latter thing if the latter is what the observer fears or expects. The one thing will usurp the identity of the other, its significance becoming like that of a metonym. This evidently happens in the mind of Carrizales. He never specifically accuses his wife of adulterous intercourse, but condemns her only by reference to what he saw (p. 44).

Carrizales shows how the unguarded use of mental dictionaries is perilous in a world in which appearances can differ from reality, particularly in situations where the reality is exceptional. Cervantes artfully does the same in the real-life context of his relationship with readers. His originality reveals the fallibility of the contemporary reader's 'dictionary' of fiction. Cervantes reveals a power of literary imagination that transcends that of the literary culture in which he operates and discloses that culture's limitations as a guide to what is possible in life and possible in artful narrative. This aspect of the novella contributes in an egotistical way to the theme of the individual's social autonomy. The author asserts his superiority in the social context of imaginative writing and his enjoyment of the social power, to surprise, puzzle and outwit readers, that his imaginative genius gives him. On a technical level his originality has a strong elitist aspect. His narrative method intensifies the novella's appeal to a discerning public in a way that slyly extends the range of his didactic interest in human relationships and makes the work a manifesto of his personal tastes in readers. The author/reader relationship becomes a test of compatibility in which Cervantes identifies the *discreto* as his ideal partner.

The core of the novella's originality is the metamorphosis of the literary source tradition: the wife's rejection of the lover, or sexual intercourse with him, and the ironical twists that follow it. These innovations do not come without some warning, for the reader is told at an early point that Carrizales will merely think that what he dreaded has happened. But the reader may forget this warning until it is fulfilled, and even if he does not forget it, the ending of the novella is a surprisingly original one. Cervantes subtly congratulates himself on his core innovation when he refers to Loaysa and Leonora as 'los nuevos adúlteros' (p. 41). An expansion of the early text, where they are called simply 'adúlteros', this description is another instance of *el hablar equívoco*. The average reader will take it at face-value, but the literal sense is a puzzling one, if only because Leonora has been congratulated for conquering Loaysa's lust, and the exemplary sense (intelligent sense) is '*novel* adulterers'; that is to say, characters who break the mould.

The phrase 'los nuevos adúlteros' complements an earlier statement which adds difficulty to the text. The earlier statement is an ominous one in which Cervantes confirms the *dueña*'s success in acting as Loaysa's procuress: 'Leonora se rindió, Leonora se engañó y Leonora se perdió, dando en tierra con todas las prevenciones del discreto Carrizales, que dormía el sueño de la muerte de su honra' (p. 40). These words are relics of the early novella which must become a stumbling-block in the revised version and one from which the average reader surely cannot recover. By triggering the usual preconceptions of what *rendirse*, *engañarse* and *perderse* mean in a sexual context with a female subject, and by announcing the 'death' of the husband's honour, the statement deceives a careless reader who forgets the prediction that Carrizales will merely imagine that his fears have come to fruition; and it would confuse a reader who had not forgotten this early warning – including the *discreto* reader – because a seventeenth-century public would expect an author-narrator to be consistent. Whether readers forget or remember the early prediction, the preamble to the succint account of Leonora's moral victory transforms convention – the reliability of third-person narrators, and the plot conventions of the type of tale that Cervantes is reworking – into a banana-skin. When the narrative has moved on, and perhaps as soon as it records the heroine's moral victory, the discerning reader will shrewdly realise that Cervantes concealed his meaning. That is to say, it will dawn upon him that he was really alluding to the predicted misunderstanding, the effects of which are just as serious as those of real adultery would have been. The discerning reader will also realise why the author has led him astray. By allowing them to read a presumptuous meaning into a statement, Cervantes has outwitted his public in one way or another, discredited preconceptions, and affirmed to the discerning few his will and ability to place his work outside the mental dictionary of literary styles; in other words, to do as he wishes despite the norms and conventions of writing fiction. Though much more arrogant, the whole procedure is reminiscent of the *burla* of the *entremés*. Both may be viewed as manifestations of artistic genius understood as the power to be 'different' in a way that somehow enlightens. In both cases, the 'difference' is an integral part of the *ejemplaridad*.

This semantically guileful passage in which Cervantes confirms Marialonso's success in the role of procuress is the third of probably five passages which increasingly tend to link ambivalence to the fictional motif of deception. The first passage is that in which Cervantes refers to Marialonso as 'una dueña de mucha prudencia y gravedad', a character sketch that is ambiguous, since its irony is unconventional by the standards of preliminary character sketches, and which an average reader might in fact take at face-value. The second passage is the second tirade against *dueñas*, where the ambivalent use of imagery might not be noted by an average readership. The fourth passage is that which speaks of the 'nuevos adúlteros'. The final and most complex passage is the authorial claim of mystification with which the novella ends.

This is Cervantes' most subtle and significant use of irony. Though the statement involves empathetic irony, which mocks a reader who wrestles with the question of why Leonora was silent, it is essentially a very sophisticated form of ambivalent irony that is based upon an authorial disguise of naïvety and simplicity. Beneath the appearance of shallowness, and partly through it, it provides a fitting conclusion to the tale as one that courts an elite, *discreto* readership, and in a sense it is an encoded signature.

It extends and recapitulates the novella's deeper significance. It completes the theme of the sovereign power of nature (Leonora was tongue-tied), darkly expresses scepticism about *libre albedrío* (her silence was a form of paralysis springing from involuntary causes), and hints that freedom should be redefined as a person's social autonomy (Leonora did not renew her pleading, much as the disguised Cervantes would have liked her to). At the same time it continues the critique of narrowmindedness. The phrase 'cuán limpia y sin ofensa' expands the dictionary of moral behaviour and the whole statement transcends the art of exemplary fiction as contemporary readers knew it. Finally, it implies that *El celoso extremeño* is a paradigmatic *novela ejemplar*. It is the virtual statement of an ethical stance in relation to readers the foundations of which are the perceptions of life that the novella itself expresses. At the same time it is a partial and very personal statement in which Cervantes asserts his ethical right to prefer one kind of public to another. Its basic implication is that writers have a natural and divine right to distance themselves from their works. Since the world is a moral testing-ground, significant fiction that is morally lifelike confers responsibility upon its readers; it tests their will to understand it and their ability to employ the appropriate moral and intellectual virtues. However, this does not mean that ethical fiction must be egalitarian. Ingenious, *engañoso*, and achieving an intense compression of meaning, Cervantes' statement patently courts a superior public in accordance with the author's personal tastes in a world in which literature, like everything else, is affected by the diversity of human nature. Its primary significance for *entendidos* is that Cervantes is a disingenuous author who is deliberately testing his public's ability to fathom exemplary characterisation and generally to transcend the surface level on which he has explained the fiction. Its secondary significance is that he and they, as readers who understand him in depth, are partners in an elite relationship which is exemplary in itself, embodying a universal truth that is reflected within the fiction: the truth that partnership, in its genuine, secure and most fruitful form, is a union of a vocational kind between two people with compatible dispositions.

The final sentence can therefore be viewed as an object lesson in the nature of literary communication understood as a communion of minds in a world in which people are different – itself understood, we can reasonably surmise, as a world that is deterministic. To those who can understand it, it emphatically declares that meaning cannot be divorced from the author or interpretation from the reader. It confirms that the absolute locus of truth is not the work but the mind that lies behind it, and that readers' responses are ultimately signs of how well they can relate to that mind. In other words, in his deliberately self-assertive way, Cervantes shows what communication must always be in the end: as English puts it, 'mutual understanding' or 'comprehension'; or as modern Spanish expressively puts it: *compenetración.*

NOTES TO THE INTRODUCTION

1. Noblemen could style themselves *don*. Cervantes appears to have foregone this privilege. The term *hidalgo* covered all levels of nobility, but the majority of nobles belonged to the petty class as distinct from the titled class. It is normally to the petty class that the term refers when used to place people in social categories. Cervantes' father proved his own *hidalguía* to the authorities.

2. 'Romance' is a modern blanket term for less realistic types of fiction with idealised heroes and heroines. Spanish usually translates 'romance' as *novela idealizada*. Pastoral romances originated in sixteenth-century Spain but were heavily indebted to the literature and ideas of Italy. They were love romances whose protagonists were idealised shepherds and shepherdesses. The pastoral setting was a literary convention connected with mythic ideas of innocence and the Renaissance philosophy of nature. *La Galatea* is in some degree a *roman à clef* and could have been influenced by a love affair that Cervantes had in Italy.

3. Though he maintained his professional links with Madrid, his marital home was in Esquivias. His daughter by Ana de Villafranca remained with her mother and we do not know if Catalina de Palacios was made aware of her existence. Cervantes' marriage was childless. The possibility that his wife was infertile must be taken into consideration when considering the breakdown of their relationship.

4. The couple lived in Valladolid from 1604 to 1606. From 1601 to 1606 this city was the Spanish capital. Cervantes' later married years were celibate. Both he and his wife took lay orders involving vows of chastity.

5. The earliest of them were medieval translations of French works some of which built on legends surrounding King Arthur. Sir Lancelot is an early chivalresque hero. The books of chivalry reached the height of their popularity in the reign of Charles V, the Holy Roman Emperor (1519-58) who was Charles I of Spain.

6. Verisimilitude (*verosimilitud*) meant 'truth to life', and in practical terms 'plausibility'. It was the basic principle in the literary and dramatic theory based on Aristotle's *Poetics* that was disseminated from Italy in the course of the sixteenth century. Neo-Aristotelians saw it as a condition of 'credibility' or what we now call the 'suspension of disbelief'. Its authority was reinforced in the second half the sixteenth century by the Counter-Reformation Church, which on moral grounds discouraged works that misrepresented reality.

7. Our information about Cervantes' earlier dramatic activity derives from the Prologue of this volume.

8. Verse had fully supplanted prose by about 1620. Two of Cervantes' *entremeses* are compositions in verse.

9.

> 'Entremés'. This is a corruption of the Italian *intremeso*, which means 'inserted' or 'interposed'; strictly speaking it is the name that is given to a hilarious play which is inserted between one act of a full-length play and the next, to enliven and refresh the audience.

Despite objections from the clergy, *entremeses* were sometimes performed at the religious feast of Corpus Christi alongside the allegorical plays, called *autos sacramentales*, whose doctrine honoured the Eucharist. Independent performances of *entremeses* took place during Carnival, the three or more days of merry festivities that preceded the season of Lent.

10. Notably *El juez de los divorcios*, an *entremés*, and *La fuerza de la sangre*, the text that precedes *El celoso extremeño* in the *Novelas ejemplares*. *El juez de los divorcios* is another work on the theme of matrimonial break-down. The action is set in an unreal Spain in which couples have access to divorce. It is essentially a series a conversational episodes in which a succession of disgruntled spouses present their cases to the 'judge'. The first of them is an intolerably shrewish woman, probably in her forties, who wants to be free of her husband of twenty-two years standing because he is now physically senile. She is tired of nursing him and is disgusted by his physical condition. In *La fuerza de la sangre* the 'unequal' couple are the parents of the heroine, a girl of sixteen, at the tale's beginning, whose brother is a little boy and whose *hidalgo* father is described as 'anciano'. A bride who married a much older man was facing early widowhood. In a typical marriage of 'unequal' partners she must therefore have married a prosperous man, or have had her own private wealth, or have come from a property-owning family (like Catalina de Palacios) which would have been capable of re-absorbing her as a widow. The groom no doubt was often a widower marrying for the second or third time. However, widower grooms may not greatly have out-numbered men who had simply postponed marriage or recanted of their bachelorhood (celibacy rates were high in Cervantes' Spain). Neither of Cervantes' two heroes is a widower.

11. Procreation was the purpose of marriage according to the Church. Moralists argued that wives needed to be young and strong in order to do the child-bearing whilst husbands needed maturity in order to be good fathers.

Differences of ten to twenty years between the ages of husbands and wives were typically seen as ideal. St Joseph was traditionally depicted as an older man in paintings of the Holy Family. This custom declined in the second half of the sixteenth century, but the distinguished Jesuit theologian Francisco Suárez could still suppose around 1600 that Joseph was thirty to forty years old when he and Mary married. Mary, he thought, was fourteen. See Pierre Civil, 'Le modèle du ménage heureux: l'image de saint Joseph en Espagne à la charnière des XVIe et XVIIe siècles', in *Relations entre hommes et femmes en Espagne aux XVIe et XVIIe siècles. Réalités et fictions*, ed. Augustin Redondo, Travaux du 'Centre de Recherche sur l'Espagne des XVIe et XVIIe siècles' (CRES – URA 1242) (Paris: Publications de la Sorbonne, 1995), pp. 21-37 (25-6).

12. *Diálogos familiares de la agricultura cristiana* (1589), ed. P. Juan Meseguer Fernández, Biblioteca de Autores Españoles, CLXI-CLXIII, CLXIX-CLXX (Madrid: Atlas Ediciones, 1963-4), CLXIX, 53-4.

13. Gilbert draws attention to Erasmus' poem 'On the Discomforts of Old Age' (1506). Erasmus wrote it at thirty-nine or forty. In it he speaks of thirty-five as the age at which old age begins its approach. He associates fifty with the likely approach of death. Erasmus' views are probably extreme by the standards of 1600, but perceptions of age do not appear to have undergone much change. Cervantes clearly saw fifty as an advanced age. The fifty-ish hero of *Don Quijote* is described by his niece as 'viejo' and 'por la edad agobiado', 'weighed down by age' (Part II, ch. 6).

14. In *El celoso extremeño* Marialonso, who is probably forty, comically claims that she is just turning thirty when she wishes to be considered young (p. 35). Other characters and Cervantes himself continue to view her as old (pp. 39-40).

15. A boy could legally marry at fourteen. Girls and boys were sometimes formally engaged to each other before the ages of twelve and fourteen by their respective sets of parents. A twelve-year-old girl might not have had sexual relations with her husband and they might not have cohabited straightaway or have done so on a full-time basis (there is some evidence that the *morisco* population – the descendants of the Spanish Moors – were more relaxed about these things), but fully-fledged wives of fifteen and sixteen were not rare. Of the eleven daughters in an ordinary family in the province of Santander who married between 1565 and 1635, six were married at ages ranging from twelve to eighteen (Molinié-Betrand, p. 244). Other studies of marriage records in different localities reveal approximately half the women marrying in their teens. The modal age of Spanish brides was somewhere in the region of eighteen to twenty-two. The majority of Spanish men married in their early to middle twenties.

16. Fathers were the legal heads of families. The widow or an older brother would normally assume the father's responsibilities if he died. Lorenza's marriage with Cañizares was possibly arranged by someone other than her father: 'diómele quien pudo' is all we are told (p. 1). Parents could not legally impose their preferences on dependent children. Nevertheless it was difficult for children to resist parental preferences since they could not legally marry in secret and could be disinherited if they did. Resistance was particularly difficult for women and they evidently came under greater pressure to marry at an early age. A woman was deemed to have failed in life if she was not a wife/widow or a nun (a 'bride of Christ') and to fulfil her traditional role as a wife she needed to have children. Furthermore an unmarried woman was a moral risk (at worst she might get herself pregnant) and in poorer families she was likely to be a burden. Note the proverb: 'Casa el hijo cuando quisieres y la hija cuando pudieres' (Correas, p. 373a), which implies that daughters are liabilities. The death of the father would probably have increased the pressure for young women to get married, especially in poorer families. James Casey, *The Kingdom of Valencia in the Seventeenth Century* (Cambridge: CUP, 1979), cites interesting examples of daughters who were married off at the age of fifteen by mothers who had been widowed (p. 20).

17. A well-known example of the first motif is the 'Bodas de Camacho' episode in Part II of *Don Quijote* (chs. 20-1), where a father prefers to marry his daughter to a rich man rather than to her sweetheart (who gets the girl in the end, though he has to use a trick in order to do so). One location of the second motif is a Cervantine *comedia*, *La casa de los celos*, that explores the subject of jealousy, both as neurotic distrust of a woman and as jealousy towards a rival. In this play Cervantes links the jealousy theme to a satire of female materialists in the *Corte*, the Spanish capital city (Madrid or Valladolid, which was the capital city from 1601 until 1606). There, so the play implies, traditional ideas of the ideal man have been banished from the female brain by economic ideas, compelling Cupid, who is one of the dramatic characters, to dress himself in fine clothes instead of going naked, and to fire arrows that are tipped with money. The play contains a satirical portrait of a *femme fatale* who puts money before charm and intelligence in choosing between two suitors.

18.

He has declared that...very old, rich men who get married for the stated purpose of producing heirs to their family names and worldly estates, when their sexual powers are at their very weakest, need to have their heads examined, because such men are not husbands to their wives but mere guardians, who spend their time stalking the figments of their jealousy.... It is also his wish to place in the self-same category of half-wits the attractive young women who marry these men in order to inherit from them. (Salas Barbadillo, *'La peregrinación sabia'* y *'El sagaz Estacio, marido examinado'*, ed. Francisco A. Icaza, Clásicos Castellanos [Madrid: Espasa-Calpe, 1941], p. 115)

The quotation is from *El sagaz Estacio, marido examinado*, a novella written in the form of a colloquy, like Cervantes' *El coloquio de los perros* (one of the *Novelas ejemplares*). Although not printed till 1620, it was officially approved for publication in 1613-14. Also of interest is the lyrical account, which could be either fiction or 'faction', of the wedding of a pretty girl and an ailing septuagenarian in the *Baile de la boda de Foncarral* (modern Fuencarral), the song of which was published in 1616: 'Casaron en Foncarral/con un viejo de setenta,/malsano de todas partes,/a una niña de perlas [...].' See *Colección de entremeses, loas, bailes, jácaras y mojigangas desde fines del siglo XVI a mediados del XVIII*, ed. Emilio Cotarelo y Mori, Nueva Biblioteca de Autores Españoles, XVII-XVIII (Madrid: Bailly-Bailliére, 1911), XVIII, 481-2.

19. In the titled aristocracy both the title and the estate were inherited by the first-born or oldest surviving son, who passed them on to his successor. The purpose was to prevent the dispersal of property by division amongst a number of heirs and to maintain the prestige of the particular noble house. The estates and the men who inherited them were known as *mayorazgos*. Some such men must have been *viejos* when they married. However, it is unlikely that they were ever elderly unless they had become childless widowers, given the weight of responsibility that rested upon them and the pressures of family tradition that they must have felt. Carrizales cannot safely be seen as a satiral allusion to this class of man alone. The ancient husbands who are lampooned by Salas Barbadillo are clearly not titled aristocrats. Described simply as 'very rich' and spoken about with frank disrespect, they are self-made men of *hidalgo* rank or commoners. Note, too, that Carrizales thinks of having more than one heir.

20. The *cabrito* was a traditional symbol of youthful lustfulness. The *cabrón* (adult goat) was a traditional symbol of the cuckold, who was also called a *cornudo*: 'Llamar a uno cabrón...es afrentarle. Vale lo mismo que cornudo, a quien su mujer no le guarda lealtad, como no la guarda la cabra, que de todos los cabrones se deja tomar' (Covarrubias, under *cabrón*).

21. In this proverb swords and women are regarded as property that the unscrupulous may be tempted to steal. The sword was a weapon associated with nobility. In social practice swords were worn by members of the plebeian classes, partly as a means of self-dignification.

22. 'Beautiful women, girls and fig-trees are very hard to guard' (ibid., p. 564a).
23. 'A woman should go out of the house on three occasions in life: for her baptism, for her wedding, and for her burial' (ibid., p. 127a). This is an unusually impudent proverb considering that regular attendance at Mass was required by the Catholic Church. Its possible sense is that in an ideal world the prohibitions on a woman's freedom would include attendance at Mass, since Mass was a communal event. The problem posed by church-attendance for a jealous husband appears in Cervantes' novella. Carrizales is frightened of it and tries to minimise risks. In the less realistic world of the *entremés*, where the wife never leaves the house, the problem is brushed aside.
24. 'Break her leg and keep her at home, and a wife will be a respectable woman. If your problem is an unmarried girl, break a leg and a half' (ibid., p. 206a).
25. Cervantes could reasonably have assumed this in the 1590s. *Comedias* and *entremeses* were almost certainly the principal vehicles of satire against the *dueña*. The rich aristocracy would have been less familiar with the theatre in 1598, when King Philip II died, than in 1613, when the decadent Philip III was on the throne. Philip III encouraged aristocratic interest in the theatre. On literary and dramatic treatments of *dueñas*, see Ricardo del Arco, 'La "dueña" en la literatura española', *Revista de Literatura*, 3 (1953), 293-343. A ridiculous *dueña* is a secondary character in Cervantes' *comedia, La casa de los celos*. Another appears in Part II of *Don Quijote.* The hero wonders if she is coming as a romantic go-between when she visits him in private (II. 48).
26. An edition of the original and unpublished version of *El celoso extremeño* follows that of the revised version in Avalle-Arce's modern edition of the *Novelas*. The early version was rediscovered in the eighteenth century in a manuscript of miscellaneous stories that also included an early version of Cervantes' *Rinconete y Cortadillo* and another novella which he may have written entitled *La tía fingida*. The compiler was a prebendary of Seville cathedral who presented the collection to the Cardinal-Archbishop (1601-9), Fernando Niño de Guevara. The early version of *El celoso extremeño* is sometimes called the 'Porras' version after the compiler's name, Porras de la Cámara. The manuscript has disappeared since the eighteenth century and modern editions are based upon the eighteenth-century printed edition of it.
27. *Llaneza* as Cervantes uses the term means simplicity of mind and manner. As an intellectual property, it is indistinguishable from *simplicidad*. Carrizales and Leonora are both described as *llano.* Leonora is also described as *simple*, and Carrizales sees his last deed (bequeathing his wife to Loaysa) as a gesture of *simplicidad.*

28. Various studies of Tuscan society in the fifteenth century have drawn attention to the pervasiveness of age-inequality in marriages made in the wealthier social classes. See especially D. Herlihy, 'Vieillir à Florence au Quattrocento', *Annales*, 24 (1969), 1338-52. This gives interesting information about weddings in Florence in 1427-8. In seventy-six cases where the ages were officially registered, the average for grooms was 33·9 years and 20·3 for brides. The average differential was 13·6 years.

29. *Orlando innamorato*, Book 1, cantos 21-2. See Georges Cirot, 'Gloses sur les "maris jaloux" de Cervantes', *Bulletin Hispanique*, 31 (1929), 1-74 (pp. 7-9); and Zimic 1996, pp. 223-4.

30. *Quanto scaltritamente Bindoccia beffa il suo marito, che era fatto geloso.* See Zimic 1967 on Bandello and the *entremés*; and Zimic 1996, pp. 224-34, on Bandello and the *novela*.

31. No one has discovered an *entremés* that foreshadows it very closely. Its nearest sixteenth-century relation is the *Entremés de un viejo que es casado con una mujer moza* (anonymous). See Eduardo Urbina, 'Hacia *El viejo celoso* de Cervantes', *Nueva revista de filología hispánica*, 38 (1990) 733-42.

32. Perhaps the most persuasive reason for surmising that the novella, in its early version, predates the play is not the one that tends to be favoured (that no writer produces the funny version of an idea he has had before he produces the serious version) but its artistic proximity to the later version of the novella. The ending of the early novella is trite when compared with that of the revised work and with the plot of the *entremés*. It is hard to believe that the latter was Cervantes' point of departure when this would imply that his second engagement with the same tradition produced a less memorable result. Cervantes could have revised the novella at any time between the late 1590s and 1612, but we may cautiously suppose that he put the early version aside till the time arrived for preparing the *Novelas* for publication (the date of the earliest censorial approval is June 1612). The *entremés* could well have been written much earlier. It appears to be influenced in minor ways by a work first published in 1602 in Milan: *La lena*, also called *El celoso* in another edition of the same year, by the expatriate writer Alfonso Velázquez de Velasco (Canavaggio, p. 162). This work was not published in Spain until 1613. However, Cervantes could have read an imported copy long before that date (Milan was a Spanish territory) and we must consider the possibility that the Velázquez influence is illusory. What seems to be a debt to him may be a debt to an earlier unidentified source that the two writers shared. More importance should probably be given to a likely link between Cervantes' *entremés* and *La casa de los celos*, a *comedia* whose versification suggests that it is one of the earliest in the 1615 collection (metrical fashions evolved considerably during Cervantes' lifetime) and whose satirical references to life in the Spanish capital city suggest a date of composition in the early 1600s, shortly after the return from Andalusia. Though the *entremeses* do not on the whole appear to have been written to suit individual *comedias*, *El viejo celoso* is a perfect match for *La casa de los celos*. The *comedia* is closely related to it through motifs of jealousy, female self-assertiveness (mainly against jealous suitors), and avarice on the part of women in attitudes to marriage. On the other hand it is stylistically very different. It takes its characters and plot material from the exotic worlds of books of chivalry, pastoral romance, and Classical mythology; it illustrates *celos* in two young and virile knights (chivalresque ideals of manhood) and a lyrical *pastor* (a pastoral ideal of manhood); it is a sumptuous spectacle play (an experiment in esthetic *engaño* that consists in making fabulous matter theatrically 'real'); and it uses spectacular forms of allegory to moralise on the subject of *celos*. The correspondences on a thematic level and the contrasting styles in character-creation and plot material (exotic/prosaic), ways of presenting moral reality (allegorical fantasy/caricaturesque realism), and theatrical styles (spectacular/ simple) would have made the *comedia* and the *entremés* ideal partners on stage. Their relationship is reinforced through common links with the literature of Renaissance Italy. The main sources of *La casa de los celos* are Boiardo's *Orlando innamorato* and Lodovico Ariosto's *Orlando furioso* (1532), its still more famous sequel. These two works are also the sources of the chivalresque characters who make an appearance in the *entremés* as figures depicted on the goatskin that is used to conceal the lover. (The characters' names would presumably have been inscribed on the goat-skin.) In a performance of *El viejo celoso* the visual reference to the Boiardan and Ariostan characters might have functioned as a humorous allusion to *La casa de los celos* and to the contrast between its romance world and the prosaic world of the *entremés*, as symbolised in the goatskin.

33. Counter-Reformation is the name now given to the response of the Roman Catholic Church to the rise of Protestantism in northern Europe. It may be dated from the middle of the sixteenth century. In Spain it entailed a tightening of existing censorship. Censors were required to ensure that publications respected the Church and were consistent with Catholic doctrine.

34. Any husband who found his wife engaged in intercourse with another man was legally entitled to kill them on the spot. But he could not kill just one of them: the double killing was needed to prove the crime. The same right was enjoyed by men who were formally engaged to be married, provided that both they and their promised brides had reached the ages at which men and women were legally entitled to marry (fourteen and twelve), at which time the engagement was legally recognised. See *Recopilación de las leyes destos reynos hecha por mandado de...Felipe Segundo*, 3 vols. (Valladolid: Lex Nova, 1982), II, 347. The law on adultery treated it as a capital crime but left punitive decisions in the hands of the offended husband. The legal rights that were granted to husbands were not extended to wronged wives presumably because a wife's position was a subordinate one and her honour depended on her own chastity and not upon that of her husband. Technically the husband's rights were rights of punishment as distinct from rights of vengeance, for in moral theology vengeance was a sin.

35. It is probably the reputation for prurience which the *novellieri* had gained that lies behind the following disclaimer in the Prologue of the *Novelas ejemplares*: 'Una cosa me atreveré a decir, que si por algún modo alcanzara que la lección destas *Novelas* pudiera inducir a quien las leyera a algún mal deseo o pensamiento, antes me cortara la mano con que las escribí que sacarlas en público.'

36. Also germane to the decency of the *entremés* is the type of dancing that Cervantes introduces at the end. See *El viejo celoso*, n. 66.

37. In its normal form this was a dramatic device that was used in *comedias* to conceal how the play would end. The dramatist would give an accurate hint about how he intended to end the play in the expectation that the audience would think he was bluffing. A Cervantine adaptation of this trick may be found in *Pedro de Urdemalas* (*Ocho comedias*) in a novel variation on the witty motif of the play-within-a-play, to which Lorenza's trick in *El viejo celoso* is also closely related. Having become a professional actor at the end of the final act, the hero of *Pedro de Urdemalas* announces that on the following day his company will perform a *comedia* which will not end with characters getting married. This can function as a concealed allusion to Cervantes' *La entretenida*, a romantic comedy that eschews the conventional romantic ending in which the characters become betrothed. He had evidently hoped that the two *comedias* would be bought by the same actor-manager and performed on consecutive days.

38. In a contemporary performance of *El viejo celoso* (though we do not know that any took place) the room would have been a curtained space beneath a gallery located at the back of the stage. This space normally served as a dressing-room but could also be used as a simple inner stage. The 'door' that is used in the *entremés* would have been either a real door located at a central point in the barrier curtains between the two pillars that supported the gallery or an imaginary door that in reality was one of the curtains. The stage would have been an open stage that projected into the audience. Scenery, if any were used, would have been very sparse.

39. The dramatic irony possibly involves a conspiratorial wink at the audience based on the use of a folk name, *Pero García*, as a code for secrecy. See textual note 62.

40. Another difference between Cañizares and Carrizales is that the former employs no staff. The only company Lorenza is allowed is that of her niece, Cristina. Leonora in contrast is surrounded by a bevy of females including hired companions of her own age. In this sense Carrizales is a more naïve man than Cañizares is. On the other hand he is not so naïve that he imagines Leonora's companions to be sexually unaware; he simply assumes that he can trust them to serve his purpose.

41. Names connected with vegetation are quite common in *entremeses*, though are usually inauthentic. The literal meaning of *Cañizares* is 'reedbeds'.

42. The woman with whom Cervantes committed adultery in the 1580s, Ana de Villafranca, had a background of this kind. Her father had placed her in domestic service at the age of fourteen in the home of one of his cousins.

43. The total length of the *Novelas ejemplares* (twelve works) is that of a single novel of medium length by the standards of Cervantes' day. However, most of the novellas are longer than a modern short story. The longest of them, *La gitanilla*, is by present-day standards a short novel or 'novelette'.

44. '¿Quién dio al pino y la haya atrevimiento/De ocupar a los peces su morada,/Y al lino [flax-plant: canvas] de estorbar el paso al viento?', Francisco de Quevedo asks in a poem of 1603 (no. 13a in Quevedo, *Poesía varia*, ed. James O. Crosby, Letras Hispánicas [Madrid: Cátedra, 1981]). The denunciation of navigation began in Classical Antiquity and underwent a revival during the Renaissance. It usually connects navigation with greed and is linked to an explicit pastoralism in its most telling manifestations. These tend to be poetic. The poet expresses his disillusionment with city-based civilisation. He typically connects it with greed, vanity, anxiety and strife. At the same time he idealises rural culture and sometimes refers to the Classical equivalent of the Garden of Eden myth: a lost age of purity and peace that was known as the Age of Gold. This broader tradition would have been psychologically present in Cervantes' novella for a cultivated reader of the time, especially one who did not belong to the wealthy social classes. The most famous attack on seafaring in Spanish literature is a long passage in Luis de Góngora's poetical *Soledades* (first published in 1627) which denounces the voyages of discovery (*Soledad* I, ll.366-502).

45. Censors attached much less importance to imaginative works than they did to doctrinal works. There is abundant evidence that their scrutiny of the former was superficial. A text that did not insult the Church, contain blasphemy or other unacceptable statement, or blatantly condone sacrilegious behaviour, was likely to receive its *aprobación*.

46. He actually promises 'sabroso y *honesto* fruto', 'delicious and *wholesome* fruit', by which he almost certainly means that the *Novelas* are sexually decent. Whilst insisting that they are exemplary tales, Cervantes gives nothing at all away about what their lessons are. He adds spice to his inscrutability by suggesting that their exemplarity has a cumulative dimension:

> Heles dado nombre de ejemplares, y si bien lo miras, no hay ninguna de quien no se pueda sacar algún ejemplo provechoso; y si no fuera por no alargar este sujeto, quizá te mostrara el sabroso y honesto fruto que se podría sacar así de todas juntas como de cada una por sí.

El celoso extremeño is an unusual novella in that Cervantes does say something about what it means.

47. In its amplest sense *discreción* is a practical virtue and not merely an intellectual one. According to a character in *La entretenida* (*Ocho comedias*) who is presented as a reliable theorist of *discreción*, it is the ability to relate to circumstance in a comprehending and therefore 'concordant' way. Its opposite is *necedad*, whose habit is 'disparity': 'El discreto es concordancia/ que engendra la habilidad;/el necio, disparidad/que no hace consonancia' (Miguel de Cervantes, *Teatro completo*, ed. Florencio Sevilla Arroyo and Antonio Rey Hazas [Barcelona: Planeta, 1987], p. 562).

48. Her love is a naïve version of the affection that all the women feel towards Carrizales before Loaysa interferes. Its sources are his liberality and congenial *llaneza*, though principally the former (p. 23).

49. The most *bobo*-like character is Luis. The central *burla* is the vow of obedience that Loaysa swears to the women. This is a parodic vow that pokes fun at the women's ignorance, though the dumb silence with which it is greeted by all but a feather-headed maid, who flatters Loaysa's eloquence, reflects not only their incomprehension of Loaysa's oath, but also the fact that they do not share Leonora's concern to protect her chastity (except perhaps for one of the maids, till she and the others have inspected Loaysa and been duly enthralled by his looks). Another *entremés* type, the black slave, reappears in Luis and Guiomar. Luis is an individualised version of this type. He lacks the *negro*'s typical gift for making music (though he tries to learn the black's typical instrument, the guitar), his red-blooded sexuality (he is an old eunuch) and his defective manner of speech. His treble voice and normal Spanish mean that he was enslaved as a boy. He was probably castrated in order to make him safe in female company. As the sentry at Carrizales' front door, he is a burlesque version of the black eunuchs who guarded the women in the seraglios or harems of sultans. Carrizales' house is explicitly compared to a seraglio at one point (p. 33). Guiomar is a more traditional character whose most typical trait is her comic manner of speech, though it is less like the diction of the typical black than that of another *entremés* type, the comic *vizcaino* (Biscayan), perhaps because Cervantes found *vizcaino* speech more comic than *negro* speech. At a murkier level than *entremeses* a range of earlier folk traditions underlie the intrigue, not all of them inherited from the tale tradition on which the plot is based. Loaysa's background includes the siren or Pied Piper type, the master of disguises, the evil magician, and the trickster who is tricked (Leonora resists him at the very moment when her virtue seems to have collapsed; and then she refuses to marry him despite her husband's Will). As a version of the trickster tricked he is related to Carrizales, a *viejo* who attempts to outwit youth only to be outwitted. Carrizales' position in the folk-tale tradition is that of the monster (powerful evil) who captures the beautiful maiden (helpless innocence). Loaysa is both another monster who fails to get the maiden and a morally parodic version of the hero who *slays* the monster, in this case Carrizales. Both characters also have a parodic relationship with Classical mythology, to which the narrator alludes. See textual notes 41 and 74. The comedy is black comedy from a moral viewpoint and probably draws on folk beliefs to reinforce the devilish aspects of Loaysa, Marialonso and their works. See Forcione, pp. 39-57 passim.

50. Aristotle expounded his theory of tragedy in the *Poetics* (also called *On the Art of Poetry* and *On the Art of Fiction*). See especially chs. 10, 11, 13 and 15. Aristotle points out that probability and necessity cannot be divorced from character: 'As in the arrangement of the incidents, so too in characterisation one must always bear in mind what will be either necessary or probable; in other words, it should be necessary or probable that such and such a person should say or do such and such a thing, and similarly that this particular incident should follow on that' (*Classical Literary Criticism*, translated with an introduction by T.S. Dorsche [Harmondsworth: Penguin, 1965], p. 52).

51. All events could be said to be 'decreed' by God. However, He did not literally predetermine human choices of any kind and He willed only the good. The distinction between things that God wills and those that He merely permits (things that are willed by the Devil) reconciles the idea of a perfect God with the self-evident reality of evil in human life. This distinction is semi-explicit in *La fuerza de la sangre*, the novella that directly precedes *El celoso extremeño* in the first edition of the *Novelas ejemplares*. See P. Lewis-Smith, 'Fictionalising God: Providence, Nature, and the Significance of Rape in *La fuerza de la sangre*', *Modern Language Review*, 91 (1996), 886-97. An intelligent reading of *La fuerza de la sangre* should attune the reader to the theological ideas that are explored in *El celoso extremeño*, but the signifi-cance of the two works is not identical.

52. Carrizales' Christian name is possibly conceived as an ironic one that

symbolically yokes him to money. If so, it defines the older Carrizales as a man who builds up treasure on earth as opposed to treasure in Heaven. As Molho observes (p. 749), Covarrubias describes a *filipo*, which could doubtless be spelt *felipo*, as a type of silver coin:

> Filipos o filipones. Son ciertas monedas de plata que se acuñaron en cierto tiempo con la efigie del rey Filipo II [Philip II]...como otras que tenían la de su padre el emperador don Carlos, que se llamaron carlines.

53. See p. 20. This must have been in Flanders or Italy at some point during his youth (p. 19). Liberality is a quality that Cervantes associates with soldiers elsewhere in his works.

54. It is worth noting that the *dueña*'s success in eroding her mistress's moral resistance is attributed to a persuasive power that may be supernatural. The things that Marialonso says are things that 'el demonio le puso en la lengua' (p. 40). This can be taken literally, as meaning that the *dueña*'s aims are now so evil that the Devil has been able to enter her.

55. Note that her love for Carrizales is a 'first love' and that a young woman's first love (that of a virgin, or *doncella*) is always the most poignant, according to Cervantes: 'el amor primero que las doncellas tienen se les imprime en el alma como el sello en la cera' (p. 23).

56. This personal God is literally a God in person, because He is an object of love. Cervantes would have known Him as Christ, God's revelation of Himself to the world.

57. A simple verbal irony is a remark in which the speaker says the direct opposite of what he or she means. Cervantes often employs such irony in the form of epithets. For example: 'el buen Loaysa' (p. 36); 'la buena dueña' or 'la buena Marialonso' (pp. 35, 37, 38, 39); 'el discreto Carrizales' (p. 40).

58. At this juncture the authenticity of Leonora's concern for her husband is to be doubted, for it is possible that she is acting. The irony of Cervantes' statement is confirmed shortly after in her response to Carrizales' revelation of his premonitions of death. The next of the extracts describes this response.

59. The ambiguity involves two possible interpretations of what constitutes the crucial moment in an attempt to resist a man who intends to have sexual intercourse, or what constitutes the crucial moment for a woman like Leonora. It raises the question of whether she could have resisted intercourse having been physically caressed. Williamson suggests that Cervantes' statement can be construed to mean that the heroine actively encouraged Loaysa to make love to her. Semantically, however, the statement hints at mere non-resistance, which it would be reasonable to regard as moral helplessness. Only Loaysa is definitely active, so *convenir* is more likely to mean acquiescent than active complicity, especially if we bear in mind Leonora's mental state as Marialonso leads her to the room. She is tearful and almost paralysed: Marialonso must almost drag her. Though this did not stop her from committing adultery in the early version of the novella, in the revised version it should colour the sense of *convenir* to the heroine's moral advantage. Her avowal at the story's end that she offended her husband only 'con el pensamiento' is a perfectly believable one, for these reasons alone (another source of credibility is the candour she displays when she admits that her husband is not obliged to believe her).

SELECTED BIBLIOGRAPHY

Biography

Byron, William, *Cervantes: A Biography* (London: Cassell, 1979).

McKendrick, Melveena, *Cervantes*, The Library of World Biography (Boston and Toronto: Little, Brown and Company, 1980).

El viejo celoso and the *entremés* tradition

Asensio, Eugenio, *Itinerario del entremés desde Lope de Rueda a Quiñones de Benavente con cinco entremeses inéditos de D. Francisco de Quevedo*, 2nd ed., rev. (Madrid: Gredos, 1971).

Canavaggio, Jean, *Cervantès dramaturge: un théâtre à naître* (Paris: PUF, 1977).

Martínez López, María José, *El entremés: radiografía de un género*, Anejos de 'Criticón', 9 (Toulouse: Presses Universitaires du Mirail, 1997).

Zimic, Stanislav, 'Bandello y *El viejo celoso* de Cervantes', *Hispanófila*, no. 31 (1967), 29-41.

El celoso extremeño and the *Novelas ejemplares*

Forcione, Alban K., *Cervantes and the Humanist Vision: A Study of Four 'Exemplary Novels'* (Princeton, NJ: Princeton University Press, 1982).

Lambert, A.F., 'The Two Versions of Cervantes' *El celoso extremeño*: Ideology and Criticism', *Bulletin of Hispanic Studies*, 57 (1980), 219-31.

Lipmann, Stephen H., 'Revision and Exemplarity in Cervantes' *El celoso extremeño*', *Cervantes*, 6 (1986), 113-21.

Williamson, Edwin, 'El "misterio escondido" en *El celoso extremeño*: una aproximación al arte de Cervantes', *Nueva Revista de Filología Hispánica*, 38 (1990), 793-815.

Zimic, Stanislav, *Las 'Novelas ejemplares' de Cervantes* (Madrid: Siglo XXI de España, 1996).

Social Background

Alcalá-Zamora, José N. (ed.), *La vida cotidiana en la España de Velázquez* (Madrid: Temas de Hoy, 1989).

Gilbert, Creighton, 'When Did a Man in the Renaissance Grow Old?', *Studies in the Renaissance*, 14 (1967), 7-32.

Molinié-Bertrand, Annie, 'Se marier en Castille au XVIe siècle', *Ibérica*, 3 (1981), 233-45.

Seventeenth-century Spanish Literature

Robbins, Jeremy, *The Challenges of Uncertainty: An Introduction to Seventeenth-century Spanish Literature* (London: Duckworth, 1998).

EDITORIAL NOTE

In editing Cervantes and, where necessary, in quoting from other antique works in modern editions, I have modernised orthography (except in headwords in Covarrubias' dictionary), expanded textual abbreviations and modernised punctuation. I have also phonetically updated words where the difference between old and modern versions is not great (e.g. *agora* becomes *ahora*, *trujo* becomes *trajo* [from *traer*], but *rompidos* does not become *rotos*) and I have introduced modern compounds (e.g. *a Dios* becomes *adiós*).

También in its archaic sense has been discarded in favour of the modern *tan bien* (as in 'dio de comer a Loaysa tan bien como si comiera en su casa') and I have signalled the archaic use of *porque* to indicate the end of an action by transcribing it as *por que*, as in 'por que su amo no le oyese'. Adjectives appear in their shortened (apocopated) form in accordance with modern usage and I have adopted modern and *castizo* use of the third-person object pronouns: *le, la, lo; les, los, las*. The archaic grammar that is left in place is sufficiently different from present-day Spanish to expose the student to little risk of confusing old and modern.

Below is a list of the archaic forms that most frequently occur in the edited texts of Cervantes:

1. *Dél, della, dellos,* and *dellas* instead of *de él*, etc.
2. Finite verbs with pronoun suffixes. Most of these are verbs in the preterite tense, though other tenses occur; e.g. *habíase muerto, parecíale, encerraréla*. I have observed the convention of conserving superfluous accents.
3. Future subjunctives , (*-iere, -are*), as in: 'si señor los viere' or 'cuando se lo mandaren'.

More likely to startle the novice reader are the following:

1. Use of verbs in the second-person plural form with singular sense, and with *vos* as the subject pronoun. For example: 'procurad vos tomar las llaves' (Loaysa addressing Luis).
2. Plural forms of the second-person imperfect indicative, imperfect subjunctive, or future subjunctive with terminations in *-des*. For example: '¿Con quién hablábades [hablabais], doña Lorenza?'; or 'No querría que tuviésedes [tuvieseis] algún soliloquio...'; or 'no dejéis de venir a cantar aquí las noches que tardáredes [tardareis] en traer...'.

3. Verb forms like *pensallo, merecello* and *decille*, which are versions of the infinitive: *pensarlo, merecerlo, decirle.*

4. Relative *quien* used in a plural sense and to refer both to people and to things, as in: 'si a todas las vecinas de quien yo pienso mal'; or 'pocos días se pasaban sin hacer mil cosas a quien la miel y el azúcar hacen sabrosas'.

Less frequent archaic forms and uses that might trouble the unprepared reader have been dealt with in textual notes.

ENTREMÉS DEL VIEJO CELOSO

Salen doña Lorenza y Cristina, su criada, y Hortigosa, su vecina[1]

LORENZA: Milagro ha sido éste, señora Hortigosa, el no haber dado la vuelta a la llave mi duelo, mi yugo y mi desesperación. Éste es el primer día, después que me casé con él, que hablo con persona de fuera de casa. ¡Que fuera le vea yo desta vida a él y a quien con él me casó!

HORTIGOSA: Ande, mi señora doña Lorenza, no se queje tanto; que con una caldera vieja se compra otra nueva.[2]

LORENZA: Y aun con esos y otros semejantes villancicos o refranes me engañaron a mí. ¡Que malditos sean sus dineros, fuera de las cruces![3] ¡Malditas sus joyas, malditas sus galas, y maldito todo cuanto me da y promete! ¿De qué me sirve a mí todo aquesto si en mitad de la riqueza estoy pobre, y en medio de la abundancia con hambre?

CRISTINA: En verdad, señora tía, que tienes razón; que más quisiera yo andar con un trapo atrás y otro adelante, y tener un marido mozo, que verme casada y enlodada con ese viejo podrido[4] que tomaste por esposo.

LORENZA: ¿Yo le tomé, sobrina? A la fe, diómele quien pudo, y yo, como muchacha, fui más presta al obedecer que al contradecir. Pero si yo tuviera tanta experiencia destas cosas, antes me tarazara la lengua con los dientes[5] que pronunciar aquel sí, que se pronuncia con dos letras y da que llorar dos mil años. Pero yo imagino que no fue otra cosa sino que había de ser ésta, y que las que han de suceder forzosamente, no hay prevención ni diligencia humana que las prevenga.

CRISTINA: ¡Jesús y del mal viejo! Toda la noche: «Daca[6] el orinal, toma el orinal. Levántate, Cristinica, y caliéntame unos paños, que me muero de la hijada. Dame aquellos juncos, que me fatiga la piedra.»[7] Con más ungüentos y medicinas en el aposento que si fuera una botica; y yo, que apenas sé vestirme, tengo de servirle de enfermera. ¡Pux, pux, pux! ¡Viejo clueco, tan potroso como celoso,[8] y el más celoso del mundo!

LORENZA: Dice la verdad mi sobrina.

CRISTINA: ¡Pluguiera a Dios que nunca yo la dijera en esto![9]

HORTIGOSA: Ahora bien, señora doña Lorenza; vuestra merced haga lo que le tengo aconsejado y verá cómo se halla muy bien con mi consejo. El mozo es como un ginjo verde;[10] quiere bien, sabe callar y agradecer lo

1

que por él se hace. Y pues los celos y el recato del viejo no nos dan lugar a demandas ni a respuestas, resolución y buen ánimo; que por la orden que hemos dado, yo le pondré al galán en su aposento de vuestra merced y le sacaré, si bien tuviese el viejo más ojos que Argos y viese más que un zahorí, que dicen que ve siete estados debajo de la tierra.[11]

LORENZA: Como soy primeriza,[12] estoy temerosa, y no querría, a trueco del gusto, poner a riesgo la honra.[13]

CRISTINA: Eso me parece, señora tía, a lo del cantar de Gómez Arias:

> Señor Gómez Arias,
> Doleos de mí;
> Soy niña y muchacha,
> Nunca en tal me vi.[14]

LORENZA: Algún espíritu malo debe de hablar en ti, sobrina, según las cosas que dices.

CRISTINA: Yo no sé quién habla, pero yo sé que haría todo aquello que la señora Hortigosa ha dicho, sin faltar punto.

LORENZA: ¿Y la honra, sobrina?

CRISTINA: ¿Y el holgarnos, tía?

LORENZA: ¿Y si se sabe?

CRISTINA: ¿Y si no se sabe?

LORENZA: Y ¿quién me asegurará a mí que no se sepa?

HORTIGOSA: ¿Quién? La buena diligencia, la sagacidad, la industria, y sobre todo el buen ánimo y mis trazas.

CRISTINA: Mire, señora Hortigosa, tráiganosle galán, limpio, desenvuelto, un poco atrevido y sobre todo, mozo.

HORTIGOSA: Todas esas partes tiene el que he propuesto, y otras dos más: que es rico y liberal.

LORENZA: Que no quiero riquezas, señora Hortigosa; que me sobran las joyas y me ponen en confusión las diferencias de colores de mis muchos vestidos. Hasta eso no tengo que desear, que Dios le dé salud a Cañizares. Más vestida me tiene que un palmito,[15] y con más joyas que la vidriera de un platero rico. No me clavara él las ventanas, cerrara las puertas, visitara a todas horas la casa, desterrara della los gatos y los perros, solamente porque tienen nombre de varón; que a trueco de que no hiciera esto y otras cosas no vistas en materia de recato, yo le perdonara sus dádivas y mercedes.[16]

HORTIGOSA: ¿Que tan celoso es?

LORENZA: ¡Digo![17] Que le vendían el otro día una tapicería a bonísimo precio,

2

y por ser de figuras no la quiso, y compró otra de verduras[18] por mayor precio, aunque no era tan buena. Siete puertas hay antes que se llegue a mi aposento, fuera de la puerta de la calle, y las llaves no me ha sido posible averiguar dónde las esconde de noche.

CRISTINA: Tía, la llave de loba creo que se la pone entre las faldas de la camisa.

LORENZA: No lo creas, sobrina; que yo duermo con él, y jamás le he visto ni sentido que tenga llave alguna.[19]

CRISTINA: Y más que toda la noche anda como trasgo[20] por toda la casa; y si acaso dan alguna música en la calle, les tira de pedradas por que se vayan. ¡Es un malo, es un brujo, es un viejo! Que no tengo más que decir.

LORENZA: Señora Hortigosa, váyase, no venga el gruñidor y la halle conmigo, que sería echarlo a perder todo; y lo que ha de hacer, hágalo luego; que estoy tan aburrida que no me falta sino echarme una soga al cuello, por salir de tan mala vida.

HORTIGOSA: Quizá con ésta que ahora se comenzará, se le quitará toda esa mala gana y le vendrá otra más saludable y que más la contente.

CRISTINA: Así suceda, aunque me costase a mí un dedo de la mano. Que quiero mucho a mi señora tía, y me muero de verla tan pensativa y angustiada en poder deste viejo, y ¡reviejo!, y ¡más que viejo! Y no me puedo hartar de decille ¡viejo!

LORENZA: Pues en verdad que te quiere bien, Cristina.

CRISTINA: ¿Deja por eso de ser viejo? Cuanto más, que yo he oído decir que siempre los viejos son amigos de niñas.

HORTIGOSA: Así es la verdad, Cristina, y adiós; que en acabando de comer, doy la vuelta. Vuestra merced esté muy en lo que dejamos concertado, y verá cómo salimos y entramos bien en ello.

CRISTINA: Señora Hortigosa, hágame merced de traerme a mí un frailecico[21] pequeñito, con quien yo me huelgue.

HORTIGOSA: Yo se le traeré a la niña pintado.[22]

CRISTINA: ¡Que no le quiero pintado, sino vivo, vivo, chiquito como unas perlas!

LORENZA: ¿Y si le ve tío?

CRISTINA: Diréle yo que es un duende,[23] y tendrá dél miedo, y holgaréme yo.

HORTIGOSA: Digo que yo le traeré, y adiós.

Vase Hortigosa

CRISTINA: Mire, tía, si Hortigosa trae al galán y a mi frailecico, y si señor los viere, no tenemos más que hacer sino cogerle entre todos y ahogarle, y echarle en el pozo o enterrarle en la caballeriza.

3

LORENZA: Tal eres tú que creo lo harías mejor que lo dices.

CRISTINA: Pues no sea el viejo celoso, y déjenos vivir en paz; pues no le hacemos mal alguno, y vivimos como unas santas.

Éntranse[24]
Entran Cañizares, viejo, y un compadre suyo

CAÑIZARES: Señor compadre, señor compadre, el setentón que se casa con quince o carece de entendimiento o tiene gana de visitar el otro mundo lo más presto que le sea posible. Apenas me casé con doña Lorencica, pensando tener en ella compañía y regalo, y persona que se hallase en mi cabecera y me cerrase los ojos al tiempo de mi muerte, cuando me embistieron una turbamulta de trabajos y desasosiegos. Tenía casa, y busqué casar; estaba posado, y desposéme.[25]

COMPADRE: Compadre, error fue, pero no muy grande; porque, según el dicho del Apóstol, mejor es casarse que abrasarse.[26]

CAÑIZARES: ¡Qué no había que abrasar en mí, señor compadre, que con la menor llamarada quedara hecho ceniza! Compañía quise, compañía busqué, compañía hallé; pero Dios lo remedie, por quien Él es.

COMPADRE: ¿Tiene celos, señor compadre?

CAÑIZARES: Del sol que mira a Lorencita, del aire que la toca, de las faldas que la vapulean.

COMPADRE: ¿Dale ocasión?

CAÑIZARES: Ni por pienso, ni tiene por qué, ni cómo, ni cuándo, ni adónde. Las ventanas, amén de estar con llave, las guarnecen rejas y celosías; las puertas jamás se abren: vecina no atraviesa mis umbrales, ni los atravesará mientras Dios me diere vida. Mirad, compadre, no les vienen los malos aires a las mujeres de ir a los jubileos[27] ni a las procesiones, ni a todos los actos de regocijos públicos. Donde ellas se mancan, donde ellas se estropean, y adonde ellas se dañan, es en casa de las vecinas y de las amigas. Más maldades encubre una mala amiga que la capa de la noche. Más conciertos se hacen en su casa y más se concluyen que en una asamblea.

COMPADRE: Yo así lo creo; pero si la señora doña Lorenza no sale de casa ni nadie entra en la suya, ¿de qué vive descontento mi compadre?

CAÑIZARES: De que no pasará mucho tiempo en que no caiga Lorencica en lo que le falta; que será un mal caso, y tan malo que en sólo pensallo lo temo, y de temerlo me desespero, y de desesperarme vivo con disgusto.

COMPADRE: Y con razón se puede tener ese temor, porque las mujeres querrían gozar enteros los frutos del matrimonio.

CAÑIZARES: La mía los goza doblados.[28]

4

COMPADRE: Ahí está el daño, señor compadre.

CAÑIZARES: No, no, ni por pienso; porque es más simple Lorencica que una paloma, y hasta ahora no entiende nada desas filaterías;[29] y adiós, señor compadre, que me quiero entrar en casa.

COMPADRE: Yo quiero entrar allá, y ver a mi señora Lorenza.

CAÑIZARES: Habéis de saber, compadre, que los antiguos latinos usaban de un refrán que decía: *Amicus usque ad aras*, que quiere decir: «El amigo, hasta el altar», infiriendo que el amigo ha de hacer por su amigo todo aquello que no fuere contra Dios. Y yo digo que mi amigo *usque ad portam*, hasta la puerta; que ninguno ha de pasar mis quicios. Y adiós, señor compadre; y perdóneme.

Éntrase Cañizares

COMPADRE: En mi vida he visto hombre más recatado, ni más celoso, ni más impertinente.[30] Pero éste es de aquellos que traen la soga arrastrando[31] y de los que siempre vienen a morir del mal que temen.

Éntrase el Compadre
Salen doña Lorenza y Cristina

CRISTINA: Tía, mucho tarda tío, y más tarda Hortigosa.

LORENZA: Más que nunca él acá viniese, ni ella tampoco, porque él me enfada, y ella me tiene confusa.

CRISTINA: Todo es probar, señora tía; y cuando no saliere bien, darle del codo.[32]

LORENZA: ¡Ay, sobrina! Que estas cosas o yo sé poco o sé que todo el daño está en probarlas.

CRISTINA: A fe, señora tía, que tiene poco ánimo, y que, si yo fuera de su edad, que no me espantaran hombres armados.

LORENZA: Otra vez torno a decir, y diré cien mil veces, que Satanás habla en tu boca. Mas, ¡ay! ¿Cómo se ha entrado señor?

CRISTINA: Debe de haber abierto con la llave maestra.

LORENZA: Encomiendo yo al diablo sus maestrías y sus llaves.

Entra Cañizares

CAÑIZARES: ¿Con quién hablábades, doña Lorenza?

LORENZA: Con Cristinica hablaba.

CAÑIZARES: Miradlo bien, doña Lorenza.

LORENZA: Digo que hablaba con Cristinica. ¿Con quién había de hablar? ¿Tengo yo, por ventura, con quién?

CAÑIZARES: No querría que tuviésedes algún soliloquio con vos misma que redundase en mi perjuicio.

LORENZA: Ni entiendo esos circunloquios que decís, ni aun los quiero entender; y tengamos la fiesta en paz.[33]

CAÑIZARES: Ni aun las vísperas no querría yo tener en guerra con vos. Pero ¿quién llama a aquella puerta con tanta prisa? Mira, Cristinica, quién es, y si es pobre, dale limosna y despídele.

CRISTINA: ¿Quién está ahí?

HORTIGOSA: La vecina Hortigosa es, señora Cristina.

CAÑIZARES: ¿Hortigosa y vecina? ¡Dios sea conmigo! Pregúntale, Cristina, lo que quiere, y dáselo, con condición que no atraviese esos umbrales.

CRISTINA: ¿Y qué quiere, señora vecina?

CAÑIZARES: El nombre de vecina me turba y sobresalta. Llámala por su propio nombre, Cristina.

CRISTINA: Responda: ¿y qué quiere, señora Hortigosa?

HORTIGOSA: Al señor Cañizares quiero suplicar un poco en que me va la honra, la vida y el alma.

CAÑIZARES: Decidle, sobrina, a esa señora que a mí me va todo eso y más en que no entre acá dentro.

LORENZA: ¡Jesús, y qué condición tan extravagante! ¿Aquí no estoy delante de vos? ¿Hanme de comer de ojo? ¿Hanme de llevar por los aires?

CAÑIZARES: Entre con cien mil Bercebuyes,[34] pues vos lo queréis.

CRISTINA: Entre, señora vecina.

CAÑIZARES: ¡Nombre fatal para mí es el de vecina!

Entra Hortigosa, y trae un guadamecí,[35] y en las pieles de las cuatro esquinas han de venir pintados Rodamonte, Mandricardo, Rugero y Gradaso;[36] y Rodamonte venga pintado como arrebozado[37]

HORTIGOSA: Señor mío de mi alma, movida e incitada de la buena fama de vuestra merced, de su gran caridad y de sus muchas limosnas, me he atrevido de venir a suplicar a vuestra merced me haga tanta merced, caridad y limosna y buena obra de comprarme este guadamecí, porque tengo un hijo preso por unas heridas que dio a un tundidor,[38] y ha mandado la justicia que declare el cirujano, y no tengo con qué pagalle, y corre peligro no le echen otros embargos,[39] que podrían ser muchos, a causa que es muy travieso mi hijo; y querría echarle hoy o mañana, si fuese posible, de la cárcel. La obra es buena, el guadamecí nuevo, y con todo eso lo daré por lo que vuestra merced quisiere darme por él; que en más está la monta, y como esas cosas he perdido yo en esta vida.[40] Tenga vuestra merced desa punta, señora mía, y descojámoslo, por que no vea el señor Cañizares que hay engaño en mis palabras. Alce más, señora mía, y mire cómo es bueno de caída[41] y las pinturas de los cuadros parece que están vivas.

Al alzar y mostrar el guadamecí, entra por detrás dél un galán; y como Cañizares ve los retratos, dice

CAÑIZARES: ¡Oh, qué lindo Rodamonte! ¿Y qué quiere el señor rebozadito en mi casa? Aun si supiese que tan amigo soy yo destas cosas y destos rebocitos, espantarse ía.[42]

CRISTINA: Señor tío, yo no sé nada de rebozados, y si él ha entrado en casa, la señora Hortigosa tiene la culpa; que a mí el diablo me lleve si dije ni hice nada para que él entrase. No, en mi conciencia, aun el diablo sería si mi señor tío me echase a mí la culpa de su entrada.

CAÑIZARES: Ya yo lo veo, sobrina, que la señora Hortigosa tiene la culpa; pero no hay de qué maravillarse, porque ella no sabe mi condición, ni cuán enemigo soy de aquestas pinturas.

LORENZA: Por las pinturas lo dice, Cristinica, y no por otra cosa.

CRISTINA: Pues por esas digo yo. ¡Ay, Dios sea conmigo! Vuelto se me ha el ánima al cuerpo, que ya andaba por los aires.

LORENZA: ¡Quemado vea yo ese pico de once varas![43] En fin, quien con muchachos se acuesta, etc.[44]

CRISTINA: ¡Ay, desgraciada, y en qué peligro pudiera haber puesto toda esta baraja![45]

CAÑIZARES: Señora Hortigosa, yo no soy amigo de figuras rebozadas ni por rebozar. Tome este doblón,[46] con el cual podrá remediar su necesidad, y váyase de mi casa lo más presto que pudiere; y ha de ser luego; y llévese su guadamecí.

HORTIGOSA: Viva vuestra merced más años que Matute el de Jerusalén,[47] en vida de mi señora doña...no sé cómo se llama...a quien suplico me mande; que la serviré de noche y de día con la vida y con el alma, que la debe de tener ella como la de una tortolica simple.

CAÑIZARES: Señora Hortigosa, abrevie y váyase, y no se esté ahora juzgando almas ajenas.

HORTIGOSA: Si vuestra merced hubiere menester algún pegadillo para la madre,[48] téngolos milagrosos; y si para mal de muelas, sé unas palabras que quitan el dolor como con la mano.

CAÑIZARES: Abrevie, señora Hortigosa; que doña Lorenza ni tiene madre[49] ni dolor de muelas; que todas las tiene sanas y enteras, que en su vida se ha sacado muela alguna.

HORTIGOSA: Ella se las sacará, placiendo al cielo, porque le dará muchos años de vida, y la vejez es la total destrucción de la dentadura.

CAÑIZARES: ¡Aquí de Dios![50] ¿Que no será posible que me deje esta vecina? ¡Hortigosa, o diablo, o vecina, o lo que eres, vete con Dios y déjame en mi casa!

HORTIGOSA: Justa es la demanda, y vuestra merced no se enoje, que ya me voy.

Vase Hortigosa

CAÑIZARES: ¡Oh, vecinas, vecinas! Escaldado quedo[51] aún de las buenas palabras desta vecina, por haber salido por boca de vecina.

LORENZA: Digo que tenéis condición de bárbaro y de salvaje. ¿Y qué ha dicho esta vecina para que quedéis con la ojeriza contra ella?[52] Todas vuestras buenas obras las hacéis en pecado mortal. Dísteisle dos docenas de reales[53] acompañados con otras dos docenas de injurias, boca de lobo, lengua de escorpión y silo de malicias.

CAÑIZARES: No, no, a mal viento va esta parva.[54] No me parece bien que volváis tanto por[55] vuestra vecina.

CRISTINA: Señora tía, éntrese allí dentro y desenójese, y deje a tío, que parece que está enojado.

LORENZA: Así lo haré, sobrina, y aun quizá no me verá la cara en estas dos horas; y a fe que yo se la dé a beber,[56] por más que la rehuse.

Éntrase doña Lorenza

CRISTINA: Tío, ¿no ve cómo ha cerrado de golpe? Y creo que va a buscar una tranca para asegurar la puerta.

Doña Lorenza, por dentro

LORENZA: ¿Cristinica? ¿Cristinica?

CRISTINA: ¿Qué quiere tía?

LORENZA: ¡Si supieses qué galán me ha deparado la buena suerte! Mozo, bien dispuesto, pelinegro y que le huele la boca a mil azahares.

CRISTINA: ¡Jesús, y qué locuras y qué niñerías! ¿Está loca tía?

LORENZA: No estoy sino en todo mi juicio; y en verdad que, si le vieses, que se te alegrase el alma.

CRISTINA: ¡Jesús, y qué locuras y qué niñerías! Ríñala, tío, por que no se atreva ni aun burlando a decir deshonestidades.

CAÑIZARES: ¿Bobeas, Lorenza?[57] Pues a fe que no estoy yo de gracia para sufrir esas burlas.

LORENZA: Que no son sino veras, y tan veras que en este género no pueden ser mayores.

CRISTINA: ¡Jesús, y qué locuras y qué niñerías! Y dígame, tía, ¿está ahí también mi frailecito?

LORENZA: No, sobrina; pero otra vez vendrá, si quiere Hortigosa la vecina.

CAÑIZARES: Lorenza, di lo que quisieres, pero no tomes en tu boca el nombre de vecina, que me tiemblan las carnes en oírlo.

LORENZA: También me tiemblan a mí por amor de la vecina.

CRISTINA: ¡Jesús, y qué locuras y qué niñerías!

LORENZA: Ahora echo de ver quien eres, viejo maldito, que hasta aquí he vivido engañada contigo.

CRISTINA: Ríñala, tío, ríñala, tío; que se desvergüenza mucho.

LORENZA: Lavar quiero a un galán las pocas barbas que tiene con una bacía llena de agua de ángeles,[58] porque su cara es como la de un ángel pintado.

CRISTINA: ¡Jesús, y qué locuras y qué niñerías! Despedácela, tío.

CAÑIZARES: No la despedazaré yo a ella, sino a la puerta que la encubre.

LORENZA: No hay para qué. Véla aquí abierta. Entre, y verá como es verdad cuanto le he dicho.

CAÑIZARES: Aunque sé que te burlas, sí entraré para desenojarte.

Al entrar Cañizares danle con una bacía de agua en los ojos.
Él vase a limpiar. Acuden sobre él Cristina y doña Lorenza,
y en este interín sale el galán y vase.

CAÑIZARES: ¡Por Dios, que por poco me cegaras, Lorenza! Al diablo se dan las burlas que se arremeten a los ojos.

LORENZA: ¡Mirad con quién me casó mi suerte, sino con el hombre más malicioso del mundo! ¡Mirad cómo dio crédito a mis mentiras, por su [menoscabo],[59] fundadas en materia de celos, que menoscabada y asendereada sea mi ventura! ¡Pagad vosotros, cabellos, las deudas deste viejo! ¡Llorad vosotros, ojos, las culpas deste maldito! ¡Mirad en lo que tiene mi honra y mi crédito! Pues de las sospechas hace certezas, de las mentiras verdades, de las burlas veras y de los entretenimientos maldiciones. ¡Ay, que se me arranca el alma!

CRISTINA: Tía, no dé tantas voces, que se juntará la vecindad.

ALGUACIL (*De dentro*): ¡Abran esas puertas! ¡Abran luego! ¡Si no, echarélas en el suelo!

LORENZA: Abre, Cristinica, y sepa todo el mundo mi inocencia y la maldad deste viejo.

CAÑIZARES: ¡Vive Dios, que creí que te burlabas! ¡Lorenza, calla!

Entran el Alguacil, y los músicos, y el bailarín, y Hortigosa

9

ALGUACIL: ¿Qué es esto? ¿Qué pendencia es ésta? ¿Quién daba aquí voces?

CAÑIZARES: Señor, no es nada. Pendencias son entre marido y mujer, que luego se pasan.

MÚSICOS: ¡Por Dios! Que estábamos mis compañeros y yo, que somos músicos, aquí pared y medio en un desposorio,[60] y a las voces hemos acudido, con no pequeño sobresalto, pensando que era otra cosa.

HORTIGOSA: Y yo también, en mi ánima pecadora.

CAÑIZARES: Pues en verdad, señora Hortigosa; que si no fuera por ella que no hubiera sucedido nada de lo sucedido.[61]

HORTIGOSA: Mis pecados lo habrán hecho; que soy tan desdichada que sin saber por dónde ni por dónde no, se me echan a mí las culpas que otros cometen.

CAÑIZARES: Señores, vuestras mercedes todos se vuelvan enhorabuena, que yo les agradezco su buen deseo; que ya yo y mi esposa quedamos en paz.

LORENZA: Sí quedaré, como le pida primero perdón a la vecina, si alguna cosa mala pensó contra ella.

CAÑIZARES: Si a todas las vecinas de quien yo pienso mal hubiese de pedir perdón, sería nunca acabar; pero, con todo eso, yo se lo pido a la señora Hortigosa.

HORTIGOSA: Y yo lo otorgo para aquí y para delante de Pero García.[62]

MÚSICOS: Pues en verdad que no habemos de haber venido en balde. Toquen mis compañeros y baile el bailarín, y regocíjense las paces con esta canción.

CAÑIZARES: Señores, no quiero música. Yo la doy por recibida.

MÚSICOS: Pues aunque no la quiera:

El agua de por San Juan
quita vino y no da pan.[63]
Las riñas de por San Juan
todo el año paz nos dan.[64]
Llover el trigo en las eras,
las viñas estando en cierne,
no hay labrador que gobierne
bien sus cubas y paneras.[65]
Mas las riñas más de veras,
si suceden por San Juan,
todo el año paz nos dan.
Baila[66]
Por la canícula ardiente
está la cólera a punto;

10

pero, pasando aquel punto,
menos activa se siente.
Y así el que dice no miente
que las riñas por San Juan
todo el año paz nos dan.
Baila
Las riñas de los casados
como aquesta siempre sean,
para que después se vean
sin pesar regocijados.
Sol que sale tras nublados
es contento tras afán.
Las riñas de por San Juan,
todo el año paz nos dan.

CAÑIZARES: Por que vean vuestras mercedes las revueltas y vueltas en que me ha puesto una vecina, y si tengo razón de estar mal con las vecinas.

LORENZA: Aunque mi esposo está mal con las vecinas, ya beso a vuestras mercedes las manos, señoras vecinas.

CRISTINA: Y yo también, mas si mi vecina me hubiera traído mi frailecico, yo la tuviera por mejor vecina; y adiós, señoras vecinas.[67]

NOTES TO *EL VIEJO CELOSO*

1. *vecina*: Someone who lives in the neighbourhood (*vecindad*) and not necessarily a person who lives next door.

2. con una caldera vieja se compra otra nueva: Lorenza was encouraged to look on her marriage as a means of inheriting wealth. 'Con un caldero viejo comprar otro nuevo, y con una caldera vieja comprar otra nueva. Lo primero dice la moza que casa con viejo y le espera heredar; lo segundo el mozo que casa con vieja' (Correas, p. 424a). In Cervantes' abbreviated version of the proverb, the gender of the word *caldera* no longer denotes the gender of the spouse.

3. fuera de las cruces: Lorenza excludes the crosses on the coins from her curse.

4. enlodada con ese viejo podrido: Loosely, 'lumbered with that foul old man'. Covarrubias tells us that 'enlodarse significa algunas veces casarse mal, de manera que manche uno la limpieza de su linaje' (under *enlodar*). The association of *enlodarse* with *limpieza de linaje* and thus with the racist concept of *limpieza de sangre* – a background with no Jewish or Moorish blood in it – might have made the word *enlodada* more spiteful for a contemporary public than it is for a modern public.

5. me tarazara la lengua con los dientes: 'I would have bitten off my tongue'.

6. Daca: *Da acá.* 'Give me'.

7. Dame aquellos juncos, que me fatiga la piedra: The 'stone' is a bladder stone: 'piedra que se engendra en la vejiga, *calculus*' (Covarrubias, under *piedra*). The reeds or rushes (*juncos*) are probably a medication. According to a herbalist tradition dating back to the *Materia Medica* of Dioscorides, the seeds of a certain kind of reed possessed diuretic properties.

8. ¡Pux, pux, pux! ¡Viejo clueco, tan potroso como celoso...!: *Pux* is seemingly an expression of *asco*, comparable to English 'ugh!'. *Clueco*: 'worn-out'. 'Viejo clueco' was probably a common insult. Correas lists it as an expression of *desdeño* (p. 743a). *Potroso* comes from *potra*: 'cierta enfermedad que se cría en los testículos y en la bolsa dellos. Cerca de los médicos tiene diferentes nombres, por la diversidad de especies desta enfermedad' (Covarrubias). An appropriate translation would be 'ruptured'.

9. ¡Pluguiera a Dios que nunca yo la dijera en esto!: 'Goodness knows I wish I wasn't [telling the truth]!'

12

10. ginjo: Otherwise known as *gínjol*, *ginja* and *azufaifa*: a kind of fruit, slightly smaller than an olive. **Ginjo [gínjol, ginja] verde:** A proverbial image for attractiveness: 'del que va gallardo y alegre, que va como un gínjol verde' (Covarrubias, under *ginjas*).

11. zahorí, que dicen que ve siete estados debajo de la tierra: A *zahorí* was a clairvoyant capable of seeing through matter or into a mind (Covarrubias, under *çahorí*). An *estado* was a measure of height or depth. It was variable in its precise value but was conceptually equivalent to the height (*estatura*) of a man.

12. primeriza: 'novice' or 'first-timer', but with bawdy implications that may or may not be intended by the speaker. If such implications are not intended their presence is a comic form of dramatic irony (an unwitting or accidental form of *el hablar equívoco*). 'Primeriza. La mujer que está para parir de primera vez' (Covarrubias). This is still one of its meanings.

13. la honra: *el honor*, but a less masculine term for it and a less aristocratic one.

14. Señor Gómez Arias...me vi: The beginning of a popular song: no. 324 in *Lírica hispánica de tipo popular: Edad Media y Renacimiento*, ed. Margit Frenk Alatorre (Mexico City: UNAM, 1966).

15. palmito: A cluster of edible palm-fruit. 'De uno que está con muchos vestidos decimos que está vestido como un palmito' (Covarrubias, under *palmitos*).

16. yo le perdonara sus dádivas y mercedes: *perdonar* in the sense of 'excuse'. She would gladly do without his generosity if he did not behave so jealously.

17. ¡Digo!: This should perhaps be *Digo* followed by a subordinate clause (*Digo que...*). Editors' preferences vary. My own preference makes *digo* an emphatic confirmation like 'I should say so!'. It is justified by the punctuation in the first edition, where a comma is used after *Digo*, and by modern Andalusian Spanish, in which *¡Digo!* signifies confirmation or agreement.

18. verduras: Literally 'greenery'. He bought a tapestry depicting only woodland.

19. jamás le he visto ni sentido que tenga llave alguna: A dramatic irony alluding to the husband's impotence (*llave* = phallus).

20. trasgo: An evil spirit capable of assuming human or animal form; also a poltergeist. 'El espíritu malo que toma alguna figura, o humana o la de algún bruto, como es el cabrón...dicen que suele revolver las cosas y los cachivaches de casa [pots and pans]' (Covarrubias, under *trasgo*). See also n. 23.

21. frailecico: From *fraile*: friar or monk. Possibly a boy in the care of a religious order (the nobility sometimes interned their sons in religious houses) but probably one whose parents dress him up in a habit: 'Frailecillo. El niño que por devoción se pone el hábito de alguna religión [religious order]' (*Dic. Aut.*).

22. pintado: 'pretty as a picture'.

23. duende: Another name for a *trasgo*:

> Es algún espíritu de los que cayeron con Lúcifer, de los cuales unos bajaron al profundo, otros quedaron en la región del aire y algunos en la superficie de la tierra, según comúnmente se tiene. Éstos suelen dentro de las casas y en las montañas y en las cuevas espantar... tomando cuerpos fantásticos; y por esta razón se dijeron trasgos.
>
> (Covarrubias, under *duende*)

24. *Éntranse*: The reflexive *éntrase* or *éntranse* means 'exit' or 'exeunt'.

25. Tenía casa, y busqué casar; estaba posado, y desposéme: *posado* means 'at peace'. In this context *desposarse* means 'to marry'. 'I had a house till marriage unhoused me. My lodgings were peaceful till marriage dislodged me' (Honig).

26. mejor es casarse que abrasarse: A saying derived from St Paul: 'But if they cannot control themselves, they should marry, for it is better to marry than to burn with passion' (I *Corinthians* 7: 9).

27. jubileos: Cañizares is referring to the celebrations connected with Roman Catholic jubilees: indulgences and other blessings granted by the Pope:

> La Iglesia Católica llama jubileo el año en que el Sumo Pontífice concede tan grandes indulgencias a los que visitaren los cuerpos santos de San Pedro y San Pablo, y las demás estaciones en la ciudad de Roma.... Otras gracias, indulgencias y perdones que los papas conceden se llaman también jubileos. (Covarrubias, under *jubileo*)

28. los goza doblados: A complex example of *el hablar equívoco* referring to sexual impotence. The surface meaning is 'twice over' or 'doubled', but two other meanings are involved: 'folded'; and something like 'moribund', from *doblar* in the sense of *tañer a muerto*, or 'to toll the bells for the dead', which is the primary meaning of *doblar* in Covarrubias' definition of the term.

29. filaterías: Normally 'cajolery' or 'smooth' or 'cunning words'. Here something like 'fancy ideas'. It is partly an allusion to the multivalent use of *doblados* (n. 28), though the speaker may not intend it in this way.

30. impertinente: 'mistaken', in an audacious or presumptuous way.

31. aquellos que traen la soga arrastrando:

> Llevar la soga rastrando, tener hecho por donde caiga en peligro; está tomado del perro o de otro animal que, habiendo estado atado, se soltó, y huyendo es cosa fácil asirse la soga en algún embarazo que lo detenga. (Covarrubias, under *soga*)

The implication is that jealousy invites cuckoldry. 'He's one of those fellows who go dragging a rope to his own hanging' (Honig).

32. cuando no saliere bien, darle del codo: *dar del codo* is similar here to the modern expression *mandar a paseo*. 'if it doesn't work, shove it'.

33. tengamos la fiesta en paz: 'let's cut out the fighting'. The literal sense of *fiesta* is 'holy day'.

34. Bercebuyes: 'Beelzebubs', 'devils'.

35. guadamecí: Also *guadamecil* and *guadamacil*. A goat-skin with pictures imprinted on it, usually hung on walls.

36. Rodomonte, Mandricardo, Rugiero and Gradasso are characters in *Orlando innamorato* and *Orlando furioso*, the Italian chivalresque romances by Boiardo and Ariosto. Their 'appearance' in the *entremés* is perhaps an allusion to Cervantes' *comedia*, *La casa de los celos*. See Introduction, n. 32.

37. como arrebozado: 'with his face cloaked'. Evidence that the characters' names were to appear beside their pictures; though Rodomonte's face must be partially visible in order to make his picture a dramatic one. It is that of a man engaged in intrigue and is reminiscent of the intriguing gallants in *comedias de capa y espada*: 'cape-and-sword plays'.

38. tundidor: 'cloth-shearer', 'cloth-cutter'.

39. ha mandado la justicia que declare el cirujano, y no tengo con qué pagalle, y corre peligro no le echen otros embargos: The magistrate in this cock-and-bull story has ordered the surgeon to make a statement and Hortigosa is asking for money in order to buy him off. He may fine her son a greater amount or confiscate his property if she does not produce the bribe. Officers of the law are often represented as corrupt in the comic literature of this period.

40. en más está la monta, y como esas cosas he perdido yo en esta vida: 'there's more involved here than money, and I'm used to sacrificing in such ways all my life' (Honig).

41. cómo es bueno de caída: Probably 'how good the drop is', rather than 'how full and long it is' (Honig). It would have been easier to conceal the *galán* by suspending the goatskin vertically.

42. espantarse ía: *se espantaría*.

43. ¡Quemado vea yo ese pico de once varas!: *vara*: a unit of lineal measurement equivalent to two *codos* and slightly less than the old British yard. *Pico* normally meant 'beak'. Lorenza is saying 'Curse that great big nose of yours!' or 'Curse your great big gob!'. One can still hear the saying 'No te pongas en camisa de once varas', roughly meaning 'Don't stick your nose in others' business' or 'Don't meddle in others' affairs'.

44. quien con muchachos se acuesta, etc: The complete proverb is 'quien con muchachos se acuesta, cagado amanece [wakes up covered in crap]' or 'sucio amanece'.

15

45. en qué peligro pudiera haber puesto toda esta baraja!: 'I really could have ruined our hand!' *Baraja*: literally a 'deck' of playing cards.

46. doblón: 'doubloon'. A gold coin worth two or four *escudos*. An *escudo* was worth 400 *maravedís* until 1609 and was then revalued to 440 *maravedís* (Hamilton, pp. 61, 65). One *escudo* was more than a daily wage. See *El celoso extremeño*, textual note 11.

47. Matute el de Jerusalén: *Matute* is a comic distortion of *Matusalén*: the biblical figure Methuselah who lived for 969 years (*Genesis* 5: 27).

48. pegadillo para la madre: *madre*: 'vulva' or 'womb'; *pegadillo*: an adhesive 'patch' of some sort. Hortigosa is probably offering a poultice for period pains.

49. ni tiene madre: A sarcastic retort in which *madre* means 'mother' and also a form of dramatic irony in which *madre* retains its anatomical sense. Lorenza's *madre*, in the anatomical sense, plays no part in her marriage.

50. ¡Aquí de Dios!: 'Heaven help us!', 'For goodness sake!'.

51. Escaldado quedo: *Escaldado* could be a dramatic irony alluding to Lorenza's infidelity. A *mujer escaldada* was a woman of loose morals (Covarrubias, under *escaldar*). The literal meaning of *escaldado* is 'scalded'.

52. ¿Y qué ha dicho esta vecina para que quedéis con la ojeriza contra ella?: 'And what has this neighbour said to leave you with a grudge against her?'

53. dos docenas de reales: A *real* was a silver coin worth 34 *maravedís* (Hamilton, p. 51). Twenty-four *reales* was a handsome sum, three or more times the daily wage of a craftsman.

54. a mal viento va esta parva: 'an ill wind blew that one in'. A *parva* is a heap of threshed but unwinnowed grain (Covarrubias).

55. volváis tanto por: *volver por*: to stand up for, defend.

56. yo se la dé a beber: 'I'll get my own back'; 'I'll make him take his medicine' (Honig). 'Dársela a beber, dar disgusto y dar un mal trago en satisfacción y venganza' (Covarrubias, under *bever*).

57. ¿Bobeas, Lorenza?: The first edition reads 'bobear Lorença', followed by a comma. Though *bobear* is not impossible, it is likely to be an error for *bobeas*.

58. agua de ángeles: Perfumed water: 'distilada de muchas flores diferentes y drogas aromáticas, rosada y las demás que se venden en las boticas' (Covarrubias, under *agua*).

59. por su [menoscabo]: One or more words, followed by a comma, are missing from the printed text. 'por su *menoscabo*' is the reading proposed by Asensio (p. 216n).

60. aquí pared y medio en un desposorio: 'close by, at a wedding'. Possibly 'at a betrothal', though this meaning is less likely. When used on its

16

own, the word *desposorio* normally means *casamiento* and is short for *desposorio por palabras de presente*. A betrothal was a *desposorio por palabras de futuro*.

61. Pues en verdad, señora Hortigosa; que si no fuera por ella que no hubiera sucedido nada de lo sucedido: Cañizares is apparently being sarcastic, using the word *ella* to refer to Hortigosa's soul (*ánima*) and the phrase *en verdad* to endorse her description of it as sinful.

62. para delante de Pero García: *Pero García* is a folk name and this is perhaps a saying. It is clearly some sort of guarantee and it may well be a form of dramatic irony in which Hortigosa is alluding to Lorenza's unfaithfulness and *Pero García* is a dramatic code for an audience that can be trusted with her secret, i.e. a dramatic irony in which Hortigosa slyly addresses the public. In his compendium of proverbs, Correas cites 'Pero García me llamo' (p. 464b) and equates it with 'Mesegar me llamo', which he says means 'callado', 'firme al tormento', or 'no digo nada'. He traces its origins to a character in an *entremés*: 'Tomóse de un entremés en que daban tormento a un ladrón y a todo respondía: «Mesegar me llamo», y no se le sacó más' (p. 548b).

63. El agua de por San Juan/quita vino y no da pan: A proverb meaning that if it rains on St John's day (24 June), there will be neither bread nor must (grape-juice for making wine) in high summer.

64. Las riñas de por San Juan/todo el año paz nos dan: A saying that derives from the custom of renewing rental contracts on houses on or around St John's day:

> «Riña por San Juan, paz para todo el año.» Fúndase en esto: que como por este tiempo se alquilan las casas, suelen reñir unos vecinos con otros sobre las servidumbres, de vistas, o vertederos, o pasos y otras cosas; y cuando lo averiguan en fresco, quedan todo el año en paz. (Covarrubias, under *Juan*)

65. Llover el trigo...paneras: 'When rain beats down on drying wheat/ And the tender blooming vine,/There is no farmer who can keep/His produce safe or store his wine' (Honig).

66. *Baila*: A number of contemporary *bailes* were considered to be indecent, but the song that the *bailarín* is accompanying is unlikely to be one of these dances' lyrics and the source of the moral offence they caused was dancing by women, not solo dancing by men. The dance directions in Cervantes' *entremeses* never prescribe the racier dances and probably only *El rufián viudo*, where we are dealing again with a solo performance by a *bailarín*, is designed to accommodate one. In this *entremés*, the dancer, Escarramán, is named after one of the dances that caused offence. At the end of *La cueva de Salamanca*, another of Cervantes' *entremeses*, the *escarramán* is described as a devilish dance and the heroine refuses to perform it. Two other dances that Cervantes condemns in the same *entremés* are silently danced in the clandestine party in *El celoso extremeño*. See n. 85 in the textual notes to the novella.

67. y adiós, señoras vecinas: This farewell is presumably spoken to the women in the audience.

NOVELA DEL CELOSO EXTREMEÑO

No ha muchos años que de un lugar de Extremadura salió un hidalgo, nacido de padres nobles,[1] el cual, como un otro Pródigo,[2] por diversas partes de España, Italia y Flandes[3] anduvo gastando así los años como la hacienda; y al fin de muchas peregrinaciones, muertos ya sus padres y gastado su patrimonio, vino a parar a la gran ciudad de Sevilla, donde halló ocasión muy bastante para acabar de consumir lo poco que le quedaba. Viéndose, pues, tan falto de dineros, y aun no con muchos amigos, se acogió al remedio a que otros muchos perdidos en aquella ciudad se acogen, que es el pasarse a las Indias, refugio y amparo de los desesperados de España, iglesia de los alzados,[4] salvoconducto de los homicidas, pala y cubierta de los jugadores a quien llaman *ciertos* los peritos en el arte,[5] añagaza general de mujeres libres, engaño común de muchos y remedio particular de pocos.

En fin, llegado el tiempo en que una flota se partía para Tierra Firme,[6] acomodándose con el almirante della, aderezó su matalotaje y su mortaja de esparto,[7] y embarcándose en Cádiz, echando la bendición a España, zarpó la flota, y con general alegría dieron las velas al viento, que blando y próspero soplaba, el cual en pocas horas les encubrió la tierra y les descubrió las anchas y espaciosas llanuras del gran padre de las aguas, el mar Océano.[8]

Iba nuestro pasajero pensativo, revolviendo en su memoria los muchos y diversos peligros que en los años de su peregrinación había pasado y el mal gobierno que en todo el discurso de su vida había tenido; y sacaba de la cuenta que a sí mismo se iba tomando una firme resolución de mudar manera de vida, y de tener otro estilo en guardar la hacienda que Dios fuese servido de darle, y de proceder con más recato que hasta allí con las mujeres.

La flota estaba como en calma cuando pasaba consigo esta tormenta Felipo de Carrizales,[9] que éste es el nombre del que ha dado materia a nuestra novela. Tornó a soplar el viento, impeliendo con tanta fuerza los navíos que no dejó a nadie en sus asientos; y así le fue forzoso a Carrizales dejar sus imaginaciones y dejarse llevar de solos los cuidados que el viaje le ofrecía; el cual viaje fue tan próspero que, sin recibir algún revés ni contraste, llegaron al puerto de Cartagena.[10] Y por concluir con todo lo que no hace a nuestro propósito, digo que la edad que tenía Felipo cuando pasó a las Indias sería de cuarenta y ocho años, y en veinte que en ellas estuvo, ayudado de su industria y diligencia, alcanzó a tener más de ciento y cincuenta mil pesos ensayados.[11]

Viéndose, pues, rico y próspero, tocado del natural deseo que todos tienen de volver a su patria, pospuestos grandes intereses que se le ofrecían, dejando el Pirú, donde había granjeado tanta hacienda, trayéndola toda en barras de oro y plata, y registrada, por quitar inconvenientes, se volvió a España. Desembarcó en Sanlúcar; llegó a Sevilla, tan lleno de años como de riquezas; sacó sus partidas sin zozobras;[12] buscó sus amigos; hallólos todos muertos; quiso partirse a su tierra, aunque ya había tenido nuevas que ningún pariente le había dejado la muerte. Y si cuando iba a Indias pobre y menesteroso le iban combatiendo muchos pensamientos, sin dejarle sosegar un punto en mitad de las ondas del mar, no menos ahora en el sosiego de la tierra le combatían, aunque por diferente causa: que si entonces no dormía por pobre, ahora no podía sosegar de rico; que tan pesada carga es la riqueza al que no está usado a tenerla, ni sabe usar della, como lo es la pobreza al que continuo[13] la tiene. Cuidados acarrea el oro y cuidados la falta dél; pero los unos se remedian con alcanzar alguna mediana cantidad, y los otros se aumentan mientras más parte se alcanzan.

Contemplaba Carrizales en sus barras, no por miserable,[14] porque en algunos años que fue soldado aprendió a ser liberal, sino en lo que había de hacer dellas, a causa que tenerlas en ser era cosa infructuosa,[15] y tenerlas en casa cebo para los codiciosos y despertador para los ladrones. Habíase muerto en él la gana de volver al inquieto trato de las mercancías,[16] y parecíale que, conforme a los años que tenía, le sobraban dineros para pasar la vida; y quisiera pasarla en su tierra y dar en ella su hacienda a tributo,[17] pasando en ella los años de su vejez en quietud y sosiego, dando a Dios lo que podía, pues había dado al mundo más de lo que debía. Por otra parte consideraba que la estrecheza de su patria era mucha y la gente muy pobre,[18] y que el irse a vivir a ella era ponerse por blanco de todas las importunidades que los pobres suelen dar al rico que tienen por vecino, y más cuando no hay otro en el lugar a quien acudir con sus miserias.

Quisiera tener a quien dejar sus bienes después de sus días, y con este deseo tomaba el pulso a su fortaleza, y parecíale que aún podía llevar la carga del matrimonio; y en viniéndole este pensamiento, le sobresaltaba un tan gran miedo que así se le desbarataba y deshacía como hace a la niebla el viento; porque de su natural condición era el más celoso hombre del mundo, aun sin estar casado, pues con sólo la imaginación de serlo le comenzaban a ofender los celos, a fatigar las sospechas y a sobresaltar las imaginaciones; y esto con tanta eficacia y vehemencia que de todo en todo propuso de no casarse.

Y estando resuelto en esto y no lo estando en lo que había de hacer de su vida, quiso su suerte que pasando un día por una calle alzase los ojos y viese a una ventana puesta una doncella, al parecer de edad de trece o catorce años, de tan agradable rostro y tan hermosa que, sin ser poderoso para defenderse el buen viejo Carrizales, rindió la flaqueza de sus muchos años a los pocos de Leonora, que así era el nombre de la hermosa doncella. Y luego, sin más detenerse, comenzó a hacer un gran montón de discursos, y hablando consigo mismo decía:

— Esta muchacha es hermosa, y a lo que muestra la presencia desta casa[19] no debe de ser rica; ella es niña; sus pocos años pueden asegurar mis sospechas. Casarme he[20] con ella; encerraréla y haréla a mis mañas,[21] y con esto no tendrá otra condición que aquella que yo le enseñare. Y no soy tan viejo que pueda perder la esperanza de tener hijos que me hereden. De que tenga dote o no, no hay para qué hacer caso, pues el cielo me dio para todos,[22] y los ricos no han de buscar en sus matrimonios hacienda sino gusto; que el gusto alarga la vida y los disgustos entre los casados la acortan. Alto, pues; echada está la suerte, y ésta es la que el cielo quiere que yo tenga.

Y así hecho este soliloquio, no una vez sino ciento, al cabo de algunos días habló con los padres de Leonora, y supo como,[23] aunque pobres, eran nobles, y dándoles cuenta de su intención y de la calidad de su persona y hacienda, les rogó le diesen por mujer a su hija. Ellos le pidieron tiempo para informarse de lo que decía, y que él también lo tendría para enterarse ser verdad lo que de su nobleza le habían dicho. Despidiéronse, informáronse las partes, y hallaron ser así lo que entrambos dijeron; y finalmente Leonora quedó por esposa de Carrizales, habiéndola dotado primero en veinte mil ducados,[24] tal estaba de abrasado el pecho del celoso viejo.

El cual apenas dio el sí de esposo cuando de golpe le embistió un tropel de rabiosos celos, y comenzó sin causa alguna a temblar y a tener mayores cuidados que jamás había tenido. Y la primera muestra que dio de su condición celosa fue no querer que sastre alguno tomase la medida a su esposa de los muchos vestidos que pensaba hacerle; y así anduvo mirando cuál otra mujer tendría, poco más o menos, el talle y cuerpo de Leonora, y halló una pobre a cuya medida hizo hacer una ropa, y probándosela su esposa halló que le venía bien; y por aquella medida hizo los demás vestidos, que fueron tantos y tan ricos que los padres de la desposada se tuvieron por más dichosos en haber acertado con tan buen yerno, para remedio suyo y de su hija. La niña estaba asombrada de ver tantas galas, a causa que las que ella en su vida se había puesto no pasaban de una saya de raja y una ropilla de tafetán.[25]

La segunda señal que dio Felipo fue no querer juntarse con su esposa hasta tenerle puesta casa aparte, la cual aderezó en esta forma. Compró una en doce mil ducados, en un barrio principal de la ciudad, que tenía agua de pie[26] y jardín con muchos naranjos. Cerró todas las ventanas que miraban a la calle y dioles vista al cielo, y lo mismo hizo de todas las otras de casa. En el portal de la calle,[27] que en Sevilla llaman *casapuerta*, hizo una caballeriza para una mula y encima della un pajar y apartamiento donde estuviese el que había de curar della, que fue un negro viejo y eunuco. Levantó las paredes de las azoteas de tal manera que el que entraba en la casa había de mirar al cielo por línea recta, sin que pudiesen ver otra cosa. Hizo torno que de la casapuerta respondía al patio. Compró un rico menaje para adornar la casa, de modo que por tapicerías, estrados y doseles[28] ricos mostraba ser de un gran señor. Compró asimismo cuatro esclavas blancas, y herrólas en el rostro, y otras dos negras bozales.[29] Concertóse con un despensero que le trajese y comprase de comer,[30] con condición que no durmiese en casa ni entrase en ella sino hasta el torno, por el cual había de dar lo que trajese.

Hecho esto, dio parte de su hacienda a censo, situada en diversas y buenas partes;[31] otra puso en el banco; y quedóse con alguna, para lo que se le ofreciese.[32]

Hizo asimismo llave maestra para toda la casa, y encerró en ella todo lo que suele comprarse en junto y en sus sazones, para la provisión de todo el año; y teniéndolo todo así aderezado y compuesto, se fue a casa de sus suegros y pidió a su mujer, que se la entregaron no con pocas lágrimas, porque les pareció que la llevaban a la sepultura.

La tierna Leonora aún no sabía lo que le había acontecido, y así, llorando con sus padres, les pidió su bendición, y despidiéndose de ellos, rodeada de sus esclavas y criadas, asida de la mano de su marido, se vino a su casa; y en entrando en ella les hizo Carrizales un sermón a todas, encargándoles la guarda de Leonora y que por ninguna vía ni en ningún modo dejasen entrar a nadie de la segunda puerta adentro, aunque fuese al negro eunuco. Y a quien más encargó la guarda y regalo de Leonora fue a una dueña de mucha prudencia y gravedad que recibió como para aya de Leonora, y para que fuese superintendente de todo lo que en la casa se hiciese, y para que mandase a las esclavas y a otras dos doncellas de la misma edad de Leonora, que para que se entretuviese con las de sus mismos años asimismo había recibido.

Prometióles que las trataría y regalaría a todas de manera que no sintiesen su encerramiento, y que los días de fiesta[33] todos, sin faltar ninguno, irían a oír misa; pero tan de mañana que apenas tuviese la luz lugar de verlas. Prometiéronle las criadas y esclavas de hacer todo aquello que les mandaba, sin pesadumbre, con pronta voluntad y buen ánimo. Y la nueva esposa, encogiendo los hombros, bajó la cabeza y dijo que ella no tenía otra voluntad que la de su esposo y señor, a quien estaba siempre obediente.

Hecha esta prevención y recogido el buen extremeño en su casa, comenzó a gozar como pudo los frutos del matrimonio, los cuales a Leonora, como no tenía experiencia de otros, ni eran gustosos ni desabridos; y así pasaba el tiempo con su dueña, doncellas y esclavas; y ellas, por pasarlo mejor, dieron en ser golosas,[34] y pocos días se pasaban sin hacer mil cosas a quien la miel y el azúcar hacen sabrosas. Sobrábales para esto en gran abundancia lo que había menester, y no menos sobraba en su amo la voluntad de dárselo, pareciéndole que con ello las tenía entretenidas y ocupadas, sin tener lugar donde ponerse a pensar en su encerramiento.

Leonora andaba a lo igual con sus criadas y se entretenía en lo mismo que ellas; y aun dio con su simplicidad en hacer muñecas y en otras niñerías, que mostraban la llaneza de su condición[35] y la terneza de sus años; todo lo cual era de grandísima satisfacción para el celoso marido, pareciéndole que había acertado a escoger la vida mejor que se la supo imaginar, y que por ninguna vía la industria ni la malicia humana podían perturbar su sosiego. Y así, sólo se desvelaba en traer regalos a su esposa y en acordarle le pidiese todos cuantos le viniesen al pensamiento,[36] que de todos sería servida.

Los días que iba a misa, que, como está dicho, era entre dos luces, venían sus padres, y en la iglesia hablaban a su hija, delante de su marido, el cual les daba tantas dádivas que aunque tenían lástima a su hija por la estrecheza en que vivía, la templaban con las muchas dádivas que Carrizales, su liberal yerno, les daba.

Levantábase de mañana y aguardaba a que el despensero viniese, a quien de la noche antes, por una cédula que ponían en el torno, le avisaban lo que había de traer otro día; y en viniendo el despensero salía de casa Carrizales, las más veces a pie, dejando cerradas las dos puertas, la de la calle y la de en medio; y entre las dos quedaba el negro. Íbase a sus negocios, que eran pocos, y con brevedad daba la vuelta; y, encerrándose, se entretenía en regalar a su esposa y acariciar a sus criadas, que todas le querían bien por ser de condición llana[37] y agradable, y sobre todo por mostrarse tan liberal con todas.

Desta manera pasaron un año de noviciado e hicieron profesión en aquella vida,[38] determinándose de llevarla hasta el fin de las suyas; y así fuera si el sagaz perturbador del género humano[39] no lo estorbara, como ahora oiréis.

Dígame ahora el que se tuviere por más discreto y recatado qué más prevenciones para su seguridad podía haber hecho el anciano Felipo, pues aun no consintió que dentro de su casa hubiese algún animal que fuese varón. A los ratones della jamás los persiguió gato, ni en ella se oyó ladrido de perro; todos eran del género femenino. De día pensaba, de noche no dormía; él era la ronda y centinela de su casa y el Argos de lo que bien quería. Jamás entró hombre de la puerta adentro del patio. Con sus amigos negociaba en la calle. Las figuras de los paños que sus salas y cuadras adornaban, todas eran hembras, flores y boscajes. Toda su casa olía a honestidad, recogimiento y recato. Aun hasta en las consejas que en las largas noches de invierno, en la chimenea, sus criadas contaban, por estar él presente en ningún género de lascivia se descubría. La plata de las canas del viejo a los ojos de Leonora parecían cabellos de oro puro, porque el amor primero que las doncellas tienen se les imprime en el alma como el sello en la cera. Su demasiada guarda le parecía advertido recato; pensaba y creía que lo que ella pasaba pasaban todas las recién casadas. No se desmandaban sus pensamientos a salir de las paredes de su casa, ni su voluntad deseaba otra cosa más de aquella que la de su marido quería. Sólo los días que iba a misa veía las calles, y esto era tan de mañana que, si no era al volver de la iglesia, no había luz para mirallas. No se vio monasterio[40] tan cerrado, ni monjas más recogidas, ni manzanas de oro tan guardadas.[41] Y con todo esto no pudo en ninguna manera prevenir ni excusar de caer en lo que recelaba; a lo menos, en pensar que había caído.

Hay en Sevilla un género de gente ociosa y holgazana a quien comúnmente suelen llamar gente de barrio. Éstos son los hijos de vecino de cada colación,[42] y de los más ricos della: gente baldía, atildada y meliflua,[43] de la cual y de su traje y manera de vivir, de su condición y de las leyes que guardan entre sí, había mucho que decir; pero por buenos respetos se deja. Uno destos galanes, pues, que entre ellos es llamado *virote* (mozo soltero; que a los recién casados llaman *mantones*),[44] asestó a mirar la casa del recatado Carrizales, y viéndola siempre cerrada, le tomó gana de saber quién vivía dentro; y con tanto ahínco y curiosidad hizo la diligencia que de todo vino a saber lo que deseaba. Supo la condición del viejo, de la hermosura de su esposa y el modo que tenía en guardarla; todo lo cual le encendió el deseo de ver si sería posible expugnar, por fuerza o por industria, fortaleza tan guardada. Y comunicándolo con dos virotes y un mantón sus amigos, acordaron que se pusiese por obra, que nunca para tales obras faltan consejeros y ayudadores.

Dificultaban el modo que se tendría para intentar tan dificultosa hazaña; y habiendo entrado en bureo muchas veces,[45] convinieron en esto: que fingiendo Loaysa, que así se llamaba el virote, que iba fuera de la ciudad por algunos días, se quitase de los ojos de sus amigos, como lo hizo; y hecho esto se puso unos calzones de lienzo limpio y camisa limpia, pero encima se puso unos vestidos tan rotos y remendados que ningún pobre en toda la ciudad los traía tan astrosos. Quitóse un poco de barba que tenía, cubrióse un ojo con un parche, vendóse una pierna estrechamente, y arrimándose a dos muletas, se convirtió en un pobre tullido tal que el más verdadero estropeado no se le igualaba.

Con este talle se ponía cada noche a la oración a la puerta de la casa de Carrizales,[46] que ya estaba cerrada, quedando el negro, que Luis se llamaba, cerrado entre las dos puertas. Puesto allí Loaysa, sacaba una guitarrilla, algo grasienta y falta de algunas cuerdas; y como él era algo músico, comenzaba a tañer algunos sones alegres y regocijados, mudando la voz por no ser conocido. Con esto se daba prisa a cantar romances de moros y moras a la loquesca,[47] con tanta gracia que cuantos pasaban por la calle se ponían a escucharle, y siempre, en tanto que cantaba, estaba rodeado de muchachos; y Luis el negro, poniendo los oídos por entre las puertas, estaba colgado de la música del virote; y diera un brazo por poder abrir la puerta y escucharle más a su placer, tal es la inclinación que los negros tienen a ser músicos. Y cuando Loaysa quería que los que le escuchaban le dejasen, dejaba de cantar y recogía su guitarra, y acogiéndose a sus muletas, se iba.

Cuatro o cinco veces había dado música al negro (que por solo él la daba), pareciéndole que por donde se había de comenzar a desmoronar aquel edificio había y debía ser por el negro; y no le salió vano su pensamiento; porque llegándose una noche, como solía, a la puerta, comenzó a templar su guitarra, y sintió que el negro estaba ya atento, y llegándose al quicio de la puerta, con voz baja dijo:

— ¿Será posible, Luis, darme un poco de agua? Que perezco de sed y no puedo cantar.

— No — dijo el negro —, porque no tengo la llave desta puerta, ni hay agujero por donde pueda dárosla.

— Pues ¿quién tiene la llave? — preguntó Loaysa.

— Mi amo — respondió el negro —, que es el más celoso hombre del mundo. Y si él supiese que yo estoy ahora aquí hablando con nadie,[48] no sería más mi vida. Pero ¿quién sois vos que me pedís el agua?

— Yo — respondió Loaysa — soy un pobre estropeado de una pierna, que gano mi vida pidiendo por Dios a la buena gente;[49] y juntamente con esto enseño a tañer a algunos morenos[50] y a otra gente pobre; y ya tengo tres negros, esclavos de tres veinticuatros,[51] a quien he enseñado de modo que pueden cantar y tañer en cualquier baile y en cualquier taberna, y me lo han pagado muy rebién.

— Harto mejor os lo pagara yo — dijo Luis — a tener lugar de tomar lección; pero no es posible, a causa que mi amo, en saliendo por la mañana, cierra la puerta de la calle, y cuando vuelve hace lo mismo, dejándome emparedado entre dos puertas.

— Por Dios, Luis — replicó Loaysa, que ya sabía el nombre del negro —, que si vos diésedes traza a que yo entrase algunas noches a daros lección, en menos de quince días os sacaría tan diestro en la guitarra que pudiésedes tañer sin vergüenza alguna en cualquier esquina; porque os hago saber que tengo grandísima gracia en el enseñar, y más que he oído decir que vos tenéis muy buena habilidad, y a lo que siento y puedo juzgar por el órgano de la voz, que es atiplada, debéis de cantar muy bien.

— No canto mal — respondió el negro —; pero ¿qué aprovecha? Pues no sé tonada alguna, si no es la de *La estrella de Venus* y la de *Por un verde prado*,[52] y aquella que ahora se usa, que dice:

A los hierros de una reja
la turbada mano asida.[53]

25

— Todas ésas son aire — dijo Loaysa — para las que yo os podría enseñar, porque sé todas las del moro Abindarráez con las de su dama Jarifa,[54] y todas las que se cantan de la historia del gran Sofí Tomunibeyo, con las de la zarabanda a lo divino,[55] que son tales que hacen pasmar a los mismos portugueses;[56] y esto enseño con tales modos y con tanta facilidad que, aunque no os deis prisa a aprender, apenas habréis comido tres o cuatro moyos de sal, cuando ya os veáis músico corriente y moliente en todo género de guitarra.[57]

A esto suspiró el negro y dijo:

— ¿Qué aprovecha todo eso, si no sé cómo meteros en casa?

— Buen remedio — dijo Loaysa —: procurad vos tomar las llaves a vuestro amo, y yo os daré un pedazo de cera donde las imprimiréis de manera que queden señaladas las guardas[58] en la cera; que por la afición que os he tomado, yo haré que un cerrajero amigo mío haga las llaves, y así podré entrar dentro de noche y enseñaros mejor que al preste Juan de las Indias,[59] porque veo ser gran lástima que se pierda una tal voz como la vuestra, faltándole el arrimo de la guitarra; que quiero que sepáis, hermano Luis, que la mejor voz del mundo pierde de sus quilates cuando no se acompaña con el instrumento, ora sea de guitarra o clavicímbano,[60] de órganos o de arpa; pero el que más a vuestra voz le conviene es el instrumento de la guitarra, por ser el más mañero y menos costoso de los instrumentos.

— Bien me parece eso — replicó el negro —; pero no puede ser, pues jamás entran las llaves en mi poder, ni mi amo las suelta de la mano de día, y de noche duermen debajo de su almohada.

— Pues haced otra cosa, Luis — dijo Loaysa —, si es que tenéis gana de ser músico consumado; que si no la tenéis, no hay para qué cansarme en aconsejaros.

— Y ¿cómo si tengo gana? — replicó Luis —. Y tanta que ninguna cosa dejaré de hacer, como sea posible salir con ella, a trueco de salir con ser músico.

— Pues así es — dijo el virote —, yo os daré por entre estas puertas, haciendo vos lugar quitando alguna tierra del quicio, digo que os daré unas tenazas y un martillo con que podáis de noche quitar los clavos de la cerradura de loba con mucha facilidad, y con la misma[61] volveremos a poner la chapa de modo que no se eche de ver que ha sido desclavada; y estando yo dentro, encerrado con vos en vuestro pajar o adonde dormís, me daré tal prisa a lo que tengo de hacer que vos veáis aun más de lo que os he dicho, con aprovechamiento de mi persona y aumento de vuestra suficiencia;[62] y de lo que hubiéremos de comer no tengáis cuidado, que yo llevaré matalotaje para entrambos y para más de ocho días; que discípulos tengo yo y amigos que no me dejarán mal pasar.

— De la comida — replicó el negro — no habrá de que temer, que con la ración que me da mi amo y con los relieves[63] que me dan las esclavas, sobrará comida para otros dos. Venga ese martillo y tenazas que decís, que yo haré por junto a este quicio lugar por donde quepa, y lo volveré a cubrir y tapar con barro; que puesto que[64] dé algunos golpes en quitar la chapa, mi amo duerme tan lejos desta puerta que será milagro, o gran desgracia nuestra, si los oye.

— Pues a la mano de Dios[65] — dijo Loaysa —; que de aquí a dos días tendréis, Luis, todo lo necesario para poner en ejecución nuestro virtuoso propósito; y advertid en no comer cosas flemosas,[66] porque no hacen ningún provecho, sino mucho daño a la voz.

— Ninguna cosa me enronquece tanto — respondió el negro — como el vino; pero no me lo quitaré yo por todas cuantas voces tiene el suelo.[67]

— No digo tal — dijo Loaysa —, ni Dios tal permita. Bebed, hijo Luis, bebed, y buen provecho os haga, que el vino que se bebe con medida jamás fue causa de daño alguno.

— Con medida lo bebo — replicó el negro —; aquí tengo un jarro que cabe una azumbre[68] justa y cabal. Éste me llenan las esclavas sin que mi amo lo sepa, y el despensero, a solapo, me trae una botilla, que también cabe justas dos azumbres,[69] con que se suplen las faltas del jarro.

— Digo — dijo Loaysa — que tal sea mi vida como eso me parece, porque la seca garganta ni gruñe ni canta.

— Andad con Dios — dijo el negro —; pero mirad que no dejéis de venir a cantar aquí las noches que tardáredes en traer lo que habéis de hacer para entrar acá dentro, que ya me comen los dedos por verlos puestos en la guitarra.

— Y ¡cómo si vendré! — replicó Loaysa —. Y aun con tonadicas nuevas.

— Eso pido — dijo Luis —; y ahora no me dejéis de cantar algo, por que me vaya a acostar con gusto ; y en lo de la paga, entienda el señor pobre que le he de pagar mejor que un rico.

— No reparo en eso — dijo Loaysa —; que según yo os enseñare, así me pagaréis,[70] y por ahora escuchad esta tonadilla; que cuando esté dentro veréis milagros.

— Sea en buena hora[71] — respondió el negro.

Y acabado este largo coloquio, cantó Loaysa un romancito agudo,[72] con que dejó al negro tan contento y satisfecho que ya no veía la hora de abrir la puerta.

Apenas se quitó Loaysa de la puerta cuando, con más ligereza que el traer de sus muletas prometía, se fue a dar cuenta a sus consejeros de su buen comienzo, adivino del buen fin que por él esperaba. Hallólos y contó lo que con el negro dejaba concertado, y otro día hallaron los instrumentos, tales que rompían cualquier clavo como si fuera de palo.

No se descuidó el virote de volver a dar música al negro, ni menos tuvo descuido el negro en hacer el agujero por donde cupiese lo que su maestro le diese, cubriéndolo de manera que a no ser mirado con malicia y sospechosamente, no se podía caer en el agujero.[73]

La segunda noche le dio los instrumentos Loaysa, y Luis probó sus fuerzas, y casi sin poner alguna se halló rompidos los clavos, y con la chapa de la cerradura en las manos abrió la puerta y recogió dentro a su Orfeo[74] y maestro; y cuando le vio con sus dos muletas, y tan andrajoso, y tan fajada su pierna, quedó admirado. No llevaba Loaysa el parche en el ojo, por no ser necesario, y así como entró, abrazó a su buen discípulo y le besó en el rostro, y luego le puso una gran bota de vino en las manos y una caja de conserva y otras cosas dulces, de que llevaba unas alforjas bien proveídas. Y dejando las muletas como si no tuviera mal alguno, comenzó a hacer cabriolas, de lo cual se admiró más el negro, a quien Loaysa dijo:

— Sabed, hermano Luis, que mi cojera y estropeamiento no nace de enfermedad sino de industria, con la cual gano de comer pidiendo por amor de Dios; y ayudándome della y de mi música, paso la mejor vida del mundo, en el cual todos aquellos que no fueren industriosos y tracistas morirán de hambre;[75] y esto lo veréis en el discurso de nuestra amistad.

— Ello dirá — respondió el negro —; pero demos orden de volver esta chapa a su lugar, de modo que no se eche de ver su mudanza.

— En buen hora[76] — dijo Loaysa.

Y sacando clavos de sus alforjas, asentaron la cerradura de suerte que estaba tan bien como de antes, de lo cual quedó contentísimo el negro; y subiéndose Loaysa al aposento que en el pajar tenía el negro, se acomodó lo mejor que pudo. Encendió luego Luis un torzal de cera,[77] y sin más aguardar sacó su guitarra Loaysa, y tocándola baja y suavemente suspendió al pobre negro de manera que estaba fuera de sí escuchándole. Habiendo tocado un poco, sacó de nuevo colación y diola a su discípulo, y, aunque con dulce,[78] bebió con tan buen talante de la bota que le dejó más fuera de sentido que la música. Pasado esto, ordenó que luego tomase lección Luis, y como el pobre negro tenía cuatro dedos de vino sobre los sesos, no acertaba traste;[79] y con todo eso le hizo creer Loaysa que ya sabía por lo menos dos tonadas; y era lo bueno que el negro se lo creía, y en toda la noche no hizo otra cosa que tañer con la guitarra destemplada y sin las cuerdas necesarias.

Durmieron lo poco que de la noche les quedaba, y a obra de[80] las seis de la mañana bajó Carrizales, y abrió la puerta de en medio y también la de la calle; y estuvo esperando al despensero, el cual vino de allí a un poco, y dando por el torno la comida, se volvió a ir. Y llamó al negro que bajase a tomar cebada para la mula, y su ración; y en tomándola se fue el viejo Carrizales, dejando cerradas ambas puertas, sin echar de ver lo que en la de la calle se

28

había hecho, de que no poco se alegraron maestro y discípulo.

Apenas salió el amo de casa cuando el negro arrebató la guitarra y comenzó a tocar, de tal manera que todas las criadas le oyeron, y por el torno le preguntaron:

— ¿Qué es esto, Luis? ¿De cuándo acá tienes tú guitarra, o quién te la ha dado?

— ¿Quién me la ha dado? — respondió Luis —: el mejor músico que hay en el mundo, y el que me ha de enseñar en menos de seis días más de seis mil sones.

— Y ¿dónde está ese músico? — preguntó la dueña.

— No está muy lejos de aquí — respondió el negro —; y si no fuera por vergüenza y por el temor que tengo a mi señor, quizá os le enseñara luego,[81] y a fe que os holgásedes de verle.

— Y ¿adónde puede él estar que nosotras le podamos ver — replicó la dueña —, si en esta casa jamás entró otro hombre que nuestro dueño?

— Ahora bien — dijo el negro —; no os quiero decir nada hasta que veáis lo que yo sé y él me ha enseñado en el breve tiempo que he dicho.

— Por cierto — dijo la dueña —, que si no es algún demonio el que te ha de enseñar, que yo no sé quién te pueda sacar músico con tanta brevedad.

— Andad — dijo el negro —; que le oiréis y le veréis algún día.

— No puede ser eso — dijo otra doncella —, porque no tenemos ventanas a la calle para poder ver ni oír a nadie.

— Bien está — dijo el negro —; que para todo hay remedio, si no es para excusar la muerte; y más si vosotras sabéis o queréis callar.

— ¡Y cómo que callaremos, hermano Luis! — dijo una de las esclavas —. Callaremos más que si fuésemos mudas; porque te prometo, amigo, que me muero por oír una buena voz, que después que aquí nos emparedaron ni aun el canto de los pájaros habemos oído.

Todas estas pláticas estaba escuchando Loaysa con grandísimo contento, pareciéndole que todas se encaminaban a la consecución de su gusto, y que la buena suerte había tomado la mano en guiarlas a la medida de su voluntad.

Despidiéronse las criadas con prometerles el negro que cuando menos se pensasen, las llamaría a oír una buena voz; y con temor que su amo volviese y le hallase hablando con ellas, las dejó y se recogió a su estancia y clausura.[82] Quisiera tomar lección, pero no se atrevió a tocar de día, por que su amo no le oyese; el cual vino de allí a poco espacio, y cerrando las puertas según su costumbre, se encerró en casa. Y al dar aquel día comer por el torno al negro, dijo Luis a una negra, que se lo daba, que aquella noche, después de dormido su amo, bajasen todas al torno a oír la voz que les había prometido, sin falta alguna. Verdad es que antes que dijese esto había pedido con muchos ruegos a su maestro fuese contento de cantar y tañer aquella noche al torno, por que

29

él pudiese cumplir la palabra que había dado de hacer oír a las criadas una voz extremada, asegurándole que sería en extremo regalado de todas ellas. Algo se hizo de rogar el maestro de hacer lo que él más deseaba; pero al fin dijo que haría lo que su buen discípulo pedía, sólo por darle gusto, sin otro interés alguno. Abrazóle el negro y diole un beso en el carrillo, en señal del contento que le había causado la merced prometida; y aquel día dio de comer a Loaysa tan bien como si comiera en su casa, y aun quizá mejor, pues pudiera ser que en su casa le faltara.[83]

Llegóse la noche, y en la mitad della, o poco menos, comenzaron a cecear[84] en el torno, y luego entendió Luis que era la cáfila que había llegado, y llamando a su maestro, bajaron del pajar, con la guitarra bien encordada y mejor templada. Preguntó Luis quién y cuántas eran las que escuchaban. Respondiéronle que todas sino su señora, que quedaba durmiendo con su marido, de que le pesó a Loaysa; pero, con todo eso, quiso dar principio a su designio y contentar a su discípulo; y tocando mansamente la guitarra, tales sones hizo que dejó admirado al negro y suspenso el rebaño de las mujeres que le escuchaba.

Pues ¿qué diré de lo que ellas sintieron cuando le oyeron tocar el *Pésame dello* y acabar con el endemoniado son de la zarabanda, nuevo entonces en España?[85] No quedó vieja por bailar ni moza que no se hiciese pedazos, todo a la sorda y con silencio extraño, poniendo centinelas y espías que avisasen si el viejo despertaba. Cantó asimismo Loaysa coplillas de la seguida,[86] con que acabó de echar el sello al gusto de las escuchantes, que ahincadamente pidieron al negro les dijese quién era tan milagroso músico. El negro les dijo que era un pobre mendigante, el más galán y gentil hombre que había en toda la pobrería de Sevilla.

Rogáronle que hiciese de suerte que ellas le viesen, y que no le dejase ir en quince días de casa; que ellas le regalarían muy bien y darían cuanto hubiese menester. Preguntáronle qué modo había tenido para meterle en casa. A esto no les respondió palabra; a lo demás dijo que para poderle ver hiciesen un agujero pequeño en el torno, que después lo taparían con cera; y que a lo de tenerle en casa, que él lo procuraría.

Hablóles también Loaysa, ofreciéndoseles a su servicio, con tan buenas razones que ellas echaron de ver[87] que no salían de ingenio de pobre mendigante. Rogáronle que otra noche viniese al mismo puesto; que ellas harían con su señora que bajase a escucharle, a pesar del ligero sueño de su señor, cuya ligereza no nacía de sus muchos años, sino de sus muchos celos. A lo cual dijo Loaysa que si ellas gustaban de oírle sin sobresalto del viejo, que él les daría unos polvos que le echasen en el vino, que le harían dormir con pesado sueño más tiempo del ordinario.

— ¡Jesús, valme! — dijo una de las doncellas —. Y si eso fuese verdad,

¡qué buena ventura se nos habría entrado por las puertas, sin sentillo y sin merecello! No serían ellos polvos de sueño para él, sino polvos de vida para todas nosotras[88] y para la pobre de mi señora Leonora, su mujer; que no la deja a sol ni a sombra, ni la pierde de vista un solo momento. ¡Ay, señor mío de mi alma, traiga esos polvos! ¡Así Dios le dé todo el bien que desea! ¡Vaya y no tarde! ¡Tráigalos, señor mío! Que yo me ofrezco a mezclarlos en el vino y a ser la escanciadora; y pluguiese a Dios que durmiese el viejo tres días con sus noches, que otros tantos tendríamos nosotras de gloria.

— Pues yo los traeré — dijo Loaysa —; y son tales que no hacen otro mal ni daño a quien los toma si no es provocarle a sueño pesadísimo.

Todas le rogaron que los trajese con brevedad, y quedando de[89] hacer otra noche con una barrena el agujero en el torno y de traer a su señora para que le viese y oyese, se despidieron; y el negro, aunque era casi el alba, quiso tomar lección, la cual le dio Loaysa, y le hizo entender que no había mejor oído que el suyo en cuantos discípulos tenía; ¡y no sabía el pobre negro, ni lo supo jamás, hacer un cruzado![90]

Tenían los amigos de Loaysa cuidado de venir de noche a escuchar por entre las puertas de la calle y ver si su amigo les decía algo o si había menester alguna cosa; y haciendo una señal que dejaron concertada, conoció Loaysa que estaban a la puerta, y por el agujero del quicio les dio breve cuenta del buen término en que estaba su negocio, pidiéndoles encarecidamente buscasen alguna cosa que provocase a sueño para dárselo a Carrizales, que él había oído decir que había unos polvos para este efecto. Dijéronle que tenían un médico amigo que les daría el mejor remedio que supiese, si es que lo había; y animándole a proseguir la empresa y prometiéndole de volver la noche siguiente con todo recaudo, aprisa se despidieron.

Vino la noche, y la banda de las palomas acudió al reclamo de la guitarra. Con ellas vino la simple Leonora, temerosa y temblando de que no despertase su marido; que aunque ella, vencida deste temor, no había querido venir, tantas cosas le dijeron sus criadas, especialmente la dueña, de la suavidad de la música y de la gallarda disposición del músico pobre (que, sin haberle visto, le alababa y le subía sobre Absalón y sobre Orfeo[91]) que la pobre señora, convencida y persuadida dellas, hubo de hacer[92] lo que no tenía ni tuviera jamás en voluntad.

Lo primero que hicieron fue barrenar el torno para ver al músico, el cual no estaba ya en hábitos de pobre, sino con unos calzones grandes de tafetán leonado, anchos a la marineresca, un jubón de lo mismo con trencillas de oro, y una montera de raso de la misma color, con cuello almidonado con grandes puntas y encaje;[93] que de todo vino proveído en las alforjas, imaginando que se había de ver en ocasión que le conviniese mudar de traje. Era mozo, y de gentil disposición y buen parecer; y como había tanto tiempo que todas tenían hecha la vista a mirar al viejo de su amo, parecióles que miraban a un ángel. Poníase una al agujero para verle, y luego otra; y por que le pudiesen ver mejor, andaba el negro paseándole el cuerpo de arriba abajo con el torzal de cera encendido. Y después que todas le hubieron visto, hasta las negras bozales, tomó Loaysa la guitarra, y cantó aquella noche tan extremadamente que las acabó de dejar suspensas y atónitas a todas, así la vieja como a las mozas; y todas rogaron a Luis diese orden y traza como el señor su maestro entrase allá dentro, para oírle y verle de más cerca y no tan por brújula[94] como por el agujero, y sin el sobresalto de estar tan apartadas de su señor, que podía cogerlas de sobresalto y con el hurto en las manos, lo cual ni sucedería así si le tuviesen escondido dentro.

A esto contradijo su señora con muchas veras,[95] diciendo que no se hiciese la tal cosa ni la tal entrada, porque la pesaría en el alma, pues desde allí le podían ver y oír a su salvo y sin peligro de su honra.[96]

— ¿Qué honra? — dijo la dueña —. El Rey tiene harta.[97] Estése vuestra merced encerrada con su Matusalén,[98] y déjenos a nosotras holgar como pudiéramos. Cuanto más, que este señor parece tan honrado que no querrá otra cosa de nosotras más de lo que nosotras quisiéramos.

— Yo, señoras mías — dijo a esto Loaysa —, no vine aquí sino con intención de servir a todas vuestras mercedes con el alma y con la vida, condolido de su no vista clausura[99] y de los ratos que en este estrecho género de vida se pierden. Hombre soy yo, por vida de mi padre, tan sencillo, tan manso y de tan buena condición, y tan obediente, que no haré más que aquello que se me mandare; y si cualquiera de vuestras mercedes dijere: «Maestro, siéntese aquí; maestro, pásese allí; echaos acá; pasaos acullá», así lo haré como el más doméstico y enseñado perro que salta por el Rey de Francia.[100]

— Si eso ha de ser así — dijo la ignorante Leonora —, ¿qué medio se dará para que entre acá dentro el señor maestro?

— Bueno — dijo Loaysa —; vuestras mercedes pugnen por sacar en cera la llave desta puerta de en medio; que yo haré que mañana en la noche venga hecha otra tal que nos pueda servir.

— En sacar esa llave — dijo una doncella —, se sacan las de toda la casa, porque es llave maestra.

— No por eso será peor — replicó Loaysa.

— Así es verdad — dijo Leonora —; pero ha de jurar este señor, primero, que no ha de hacer otra cosa cuando esté acá dentro sino cantar y tañer cuando se lo mandaren, y que ha de estar encerrado y quedito donde le pusiéramos.

— Sí juro — dijo Loaysa.

— No vale nada ese juramento — respondió Leonora —; que ha de jurar por vida de su padre, y ha de jurar la cruz, y besalla que lo veamos todas.[101]

— Por vida de mi padre juro — dijo Loaysa —, y por esta señal de cruz, que la beso con mi boca sucia.[102]

Y haciendo la cruz con dos dedos, la besó tres veces. Esto hecho, dijo otra de las doncellas:

— Mire, señor, que no se le olvide aquello de los polvos, que es el *tuáutem* de todo.[103]

Con esto cesó la plática de aquella noche, quedando todos muy contentos del concierto. Y la suerte, que de bien en mejor encaminaba los negocios de Loaysa, trajo a aquellas horas, que eran dos después de la media noche, por la calle a sus amigos, los cuales, haciendo la señal acostumbrada, que era tocar una trompa de París, Loaysa les habló y les dio cuenta del término en que estaba su pretensión, y les pidió si traían los polvos, u otra cosa, como se la había pedido, para que Carrizales durmiese. Díjoles asimismo lo de la llave maestra. Ellos le dijeron que los polvos, o un ungüento, vendría la siguiente noche, de tal virtud que untados los pulsos y las sienes con él, causaba un sueño profundo, sin que dél se pudiese despertar en dos días si no era lavándose con vinagre todas las partes que se habían untado; y que se les diese la llave en cera, que asimismo la harían hacer con facilidad. Con esto se despidieron, y Loaysa y su discípulo durmieron lo poco que de la noche les quedaba, esperando Loaysa con gran deseo la venidera, por ver si se le cumplía la palabra prometida de la llave.

Y puesto que[104] el tiempo parece tardío y perezoso a los que en él esperan, en fin corre a las parejas con el mismo pensamiento y llega el término que quiere,[105] porque nunca para ni sosiega. Vino, pues, la noche y la hora acostumbrada de acudir al torno, donde vinieron todas las criadas de casa, grandes y chicas, negras y blancas, porque todas estaban deseosas de ver dentro de su serrallo al señor músico. Pero no vino Leonora, y preguntando Loaysa por ella le respondieron que estaba acostada con su velado,[106] el cual tenía cerrada la puerta del aposento donde dormía con llave, y después de haber cerrado se la ponía debajo de la almohada, y que su señora les había dicho que, en durmiéndose el viejo, haría por tomarle la llave maestra y sacarla en cera, que ya llevaba preparada y blanda, y que de allí a un poco habían de ir a requerirla por una gatera.

Maravillado quedó Loaysa del recato del viejo; pero no por esto se le desmayó el deseo; y estando en esto oyó la trompa de París. Acudió al puesto; halló a sus amigos, que le dieron un botecico de ungüento de la propiedad que le habían significado; tomólo Loaysa, y díjoles que esperasen un poco, que les daría la muestra de la llave. Volvióse al torno y dijo a la dueña, que era la que con más ahínco mostraba desear su entrada, que se lo llevase a la señora Leonora, diciéndole la propiedad que tenía y que procurase untar a su marido con tal tiento que no lo sintiese, y que vería maravillas. Hízolo así la dueña; y llegándose a la gatera halló que estaba Leonora esperando, tendida

33

en el suelo de largo a largo, puesto el rostro en la gatera. Llegó la dueña, y tendiéndose de la misma manera puso la boca en el oído de su señora, y con voz baja le dijo que traía el ungüento y de la manera que había de probar su virtud. Ella tomó el ungüento, y respondió a la dueña como en ninguna manera podía tomar la llave a su marido, porque no la tenía debajo de la almohada, como solía, sino entre los dos colchones, y casi debajo de la mitad de su cuerpo; pero que dijese al maestro que si el ungüento obraba como él decía, con facilidad sacarían la llave todas las veces que quisiesen, y así no sería necesario sacarla en cera. Dijo que fuese a decirlo luego, y volviese a ver lo que el ungüento obraba, porque luego luego[107] le pensaba untar a su velado.

Bajó la dueña a decirlo al maestro Loaysa, y él despidió a sus amigos, que esperando la llave estaban. Temblando y pasito, y casi sin osar despedir el aliento de la boca, llegó Leonora a untar los pulsos del celoso marido, y asimismo le untó las ventanas de las narices; y cuando a ellas le llegó le parecía que se estremecía, y ella quedó mortal, pareciéndole que la había cogido en el hurto. En efecto, como mejor pudo le acabó de untar todos los lugares que le dijeron ser necesarios, que fue lo mismo que haberle embalsamado para la sepultura.

Poco espacio tardó el alopiado ungüento[108] en dar manifiestas señales de su virtud, porque luego comenzó a dar el viejo tan grandes ronquidos que se pudieran oír en la calle: música a los oídos de su esposa, más acordada que la del maestro de su negro. Y aún mal segura de lo que veía, se llegó a él y le estremeció un poco, y luego más, y luego otro poquito más, por ver si despertaba; y a tanto se atrevió que le volvió de una parte a otra, sin que despertase. Como vio esto, se fue a la gatera de la puerta y, con voz no tan baja como la primera, llamó a la dueña, que allí la estaba esperando, y le dijo:

— Dame albricias, hermana, que Carrizales duerme más que un muerto.

— Pues ¿a qué aguardas a tomar la llave, señora? — dijo la dueña —. Mira que está el músico aguardándola más ha de una hora.[109]

— Espera, hermana, que ya voy por ella — respondió Leonora.

Y volviendo a la cama, metió la mano por entre los colchones y sacó la llave de en medio dellos, sin que el viejo lo sintiese; y tomándola en sus manos, comenzó a dar brincos de contento, y sin más esperar abrió la puerta y la presentó a su dueña, que la recibió con la mayor alegría del mundo.

Mandó Leonora que fuese a abrir al músico y que le trajese a los corredores, porque ella no osaba quitarse de allí, por lo que podía suceder; pero que ante todas cosas hiciese que de nuevo ratificase el juramento que había hecho de no hacer más de lo que ellas le ordenasen, y que si no lo quisiese confirmar y hacer de nuevo, en ninguna manera le abriesen.

— Así será — dijo la dueña —; y a fe que no ha de entrar si primero no jura y rejura y besa la cruz seis veces.

— No le pongas tasa — dijo Leonora —; bésela él, y sean las veces que quisiere; pero mira que jure la vida de sus padres y por todo aquello que bien quiere, porque con esto estaremos seguras y nos hartaremos de oírle cantar y tañer; que en mi ánima que lo hace delicadamente; y anda, no te detengas más, por que no se nos pase la noche en pláticas.

Alzóse las faldas la buena dueña y con no vista ligereza se puso en el torno, donde estaba toda la gente de casa esperándola; y habiéndoles mostrado la llave que traía, fue tanto el contento de todas que la alzaron en peso como a catedrático,[110] diciendo: «¡Viva! ¡Viva!», y más cuando les dijo que no había necesidad de contrahacer la llave, porque según el untado viejo dormía, bien se podían aprovechar de la de casa todas las veces que la quisiesen.

— ¡Ea, pues, amiga![111] — dijo una de las doncellas —. ¡Ábrase esa puerta y entre este señor! ¡Que ha mucho que aguarda! Y ¡démonos un verde de música que no haya más que ver![112]

— Más ha de haber que ver — replicó la dueña —: que le hemos de tomar juramento, como la otra noche.[113]

— Él es tan bueno — dijo una de las esclavas — que no reparará en juramentos.

Abrió en esto la dueña la puerta, y teniéndola entreabierta llamó a Loaysa, que todo lo había estado escuchando por el agujero del torno; el cual, llegándose a la puerta, quiso entrarse de golpe, mas poniéndole la dueña la mano en el pecho, le dijo:

— Sabrá vuestra merced, señor mío, que en Dios y en mi conciencia todas las que estamos dentro de las puertas desta casa somos doncellas como las madres que nos pariçron, excepto mi señora; y aunque yo debo de parecer de cuarenta años, no teniendo treinta cumplidos, porque les faltan dos meses y medio, también lo soy, mal pecado;[114] y si acaso parezco vieja, corrimientos,[115] trabajos y desabrimientos echan un cero a los años, y a veces dos, según se les antoja. Y siendo esto así como lo es, no sería razón que a trueco de oír dos, o tres, o cuatro cantares nos pusiésemos a perder tanta virginidad como aquí se encierra;·porque hasta esta negra, que se llama Guiomar, es doncella. Así que, señor de mi corazón, vuestra merced nos ha de hacer primero que entre en nuestro reino un muy solemne juramento de que no ha de hacer más de lo que nosotras le ordenáremos; y si le parece que es mucho lo que se le pide, considere que es mucho más lo que se aventura. Y si es que vuestra merced viene con buena intención, poco le ha de doler el jurar, que al buen pagador no le duelen prendas.

— Bien y rebién ha dicho la señora Marialonso — dijo una de las doncellas —; en fin, como persona discreta y que está en las cosas como se debe; y si es que el señor no quiere jurar, no entre acá dentro.

A esto dijo Guiomar la negra, que no era muy ladina:

— Por mí, más que nunca jura, entre con todo diablo; que aunque más jura, si acá estás, todo olvida.[116]

Oyó con gran sosiego Loaysa la arenga de la señora Marialonso, y con grave reposo y autoridad respondió:

— Por cierto, señoras hermanas y compañeras mías, que nunca mi intento fue, es, ni será otro que daros gusto y contento en cuanto mis fuerzas alcanzaren, y así no se me hará cuesta arriba este juramento que me piden; pero quisiera yo que se fiara algo de mi palabra, porque dada de tal persona como yo soy, era lo mismo que hacer una obligación guarentigia;[117] y quiero hacer saber a vuestra merced que debajo del sayal hay ál, y que debajo de mala capa suele estar un buen bebedor.[118] Mas para que todas estén seguras de mi buen deseo, determino de jurar como católico y buen varón; y así, juro por la intemerata eficacia, donde más santa y largamente se contiene,[119] y por las entradas y salidas del santo Líbano monte,[120] y por todo aquello que en su proemio encierra la verdadera historia de Carlomagno, con la muerte del gigante Fierabrás,[121] de no salir ni pasar del juramento hecho y del mandamiento de la más mínima y desechada destas señoras, so pena que si otra cosa hiciere o quisiere hacer, desde ahora para entonces y desde entonces para ahora lo doy por nulo y no hecho ni valedero.

Aquí llegaba con su juramento el buen Loaysa cuando una de las dos doncellas, que con atención le había estado escuchando, dio una gran voz, diciendo:

— ¡Éste sí que es juramento para enternecer las piedras! ¡Mal haya yo si más quiero que jures, pues con sólo lo jurado podías entrar en la misma sima de Cabra![122]

Y asiéndole de los gregüescos,[123] le metió dentro, y luego todas las demás se le pusieron a la redonda. Luego fue una a dar las nuevas a su señora, la cual estaba haciendo centinela al sueño de su esposo; y cuando la mensajera le dijo que ya subía el músico, se alegró y se turbó en un punto, y preguntó si había jurado. Respondióle que sí, y con la más nueva forma de juramento que en su vida había visto.

— Pues si ha jurado — dijo Leonora —, asido le tenemos. ¡Oh, qué avisada que anduve en hacelle que jurase!

En esto llegó toda la caterva junta, y el músico en medio, alumbrándolos el negro y Guiomar la negra. Y viendo Loaysa a Leonora, hizo muestras de arrojársele a los pies para besarle las manos. Ella, callando y por señas, le hizo levantar, y todas estaban como mudas, sin osar hablar, temerosas que su señor las oyese; lo cual considerado por Loaysa, les dijo que bien podían hablar alto, porque el ungüento con que estaba untado su señor tenía tal virtud que, fuera de quitar la vida, ponía a un hombre como muerto.

— Así lo creo yo — dijo Leonora —; que si así no fuera, ya él hubiera

36

despertado veinte veces, según le hacen de sueño ligero sus muchas indisposiciones; pero después que le unté, ronca como un animal.

— Pues eso es así — dijo la dueña —, vámonos a aquella sala frontera, donde podremos oír cantar aquí al señor y regocijarnos un poco.

— Vamos — dijo Leonora —; pero quédese aquí Guiomar por guarda, que nos avise si Carrizales despierta.

A lo cual respondió Guiomar:

— Yo, negra, quedo. Blancas van. ¡Dios perdone a todas!

Quedóse la negra; fuéronse a la sala, donde había un rico estrado, y cogiendo al señor en medio, se sentaron todas. Y tomando la buena Marialonso una vela, comenzó a mirar de arriba abajo al bueno del músico, y una decía: «¡Ay! ¡Qué copete[124] que tiene tan lindo y tan rizado!» Otra: «¡Ay! ¡Qué blancura de dientes! ¡Mal año para piñones mondados que más blancos ni más lindos sean!»[125] Otra: «¡Ay! ¡Qué ojos tan grandes y tan rasgados! ¡Y por el siglo de mi madre, que son verdes! ¡Que no parecen sino que son de esmeraldas!» Ésta alababa la boca, aquélla los pies, y todas juntas hicieron dél una menuda anatomía y pepitoria.[126] Sola Leonora callaba, y le miraba, y le iba pareciendo de mejor talle que su velado. En esto la dueña tomó la guitarra, que tenía el negro, y se la puso en las manos de Loaysa, rogándole que la tocase y que cantase unas coplicas que entonces andaban muy validas en Sevilla, que decían:

Madre, la mi madre,
guardas me ponéis.

Cumplióle Loaysa su deseo. Levantáronse todas y se comenzaron a hacer pedazos bailando. Sabía la dueña las coplas, y cantólas con más gusto que buena voz, y fueron éstas:

Madre, la mi madre,
guardas me ponéis,
que si yo no me guardo,
no me guardaréis.
Dicen que está escrito,
y con gran razón,
ser la privación
causa de apetito;
crece en infinito
encerrado amor;
por eso es mejor
que no me encerréis;

que si yo, etc.
  Si la voluntad
por sí no se guarda,
no la harán guarda
miedo o calidad;
romperá, en verdad,
por la misma muerte,
hasta hallar la suerte
que vos no entendéis;
que si yo, etc.
  Quien tiene costumbre
de ser amorosa,
como mariposa
se irá tras su lumbre,
aunque muchedumbre
de guardas le pongan,
y aunque más propongan
de hacer lo que hacéis;
que si yo, etc.
  Es de tal manera
la fuerza amorosa,
que a la más hermosa
la vuelve en quimera:
el pecho de cera,
de fuego la gana,
las manos de lana,
de fieltro los pies;
que si yo no me guardo,
mal me guardaréis.[127]

Al fin llegaban de su canto y baile el corro de las mozas, guiado por la buena dueña, cuando llegó Guiomar, la centinela, toda turbada, hiriendo de pie y de mano como si tuviera alferecía,[128] y con voz entre ronca y baja, dijo:

— ¡Despierto señor, señora; y, señora, despierto señor, y levantas y viene!

Quien ha visto banda de palomas estar comiendo en el campo sin miedo lo que ajenas manos sembraron, que al furioso estrépito de disparada escopeta se azora y levanta, y olvidada del pasto, confusa y atónita cruza por los aires, tal se imagine que quedó la banda y corro de las bailadoras, pasmadas y temerosas, oyendo la no esperada nueva que Guiomar había traído; y procurando cada una su disculpa y todas juntas su remedio, cuál por una y cuál por otra parte, se fueron a esconder por los desvanes y rincones de la casa, dejando solo al músico, el cual, dejando la guitarra y el canto, lleno de turbación, no sabía qué hacerse.

Torcía Leonora sus hermosas manos; abofeteábase el rostro, aunque blandamente, la señora Marialonso; en fin, todo era confusión, sobresalto y miedo. Pero la dueña, como más astuta y reportada, dio orden que Loaysa se entrase en un aposento suyo, y que ella y su señora se quedarían en la sala; que no faltaría excusa que dar a su señor si allí las hallase.

Escondióse luego Loaysa, y la dueña se puso atenta a escuchar si su amo venía, y no sintiendo rumor alguno cobró ánimo, y poco a poco, paso ante paso, se fue llegando al aposento donde su señor dormía, y oyó que roncaba como primero; y asegurada de que dormía, alzó las faldas y volvió corriendo a pedir albricias a su señora del sueño de su amo, la cual se las mandó de muy entera voluntad.

No quiso la buena dueña perder la coyuntura que la suerte le ofrecía de gozar, primero que todas, las gracias que ésta se imaginaba que debía tener el músico; y así, diciéndole a Leonora que esperase en la sala en tanto que iba a llamarle, la dejó y se entró donde él estaba, no menos confuso que pensativo, esperando las nuevas de lo que hacía el viejo untado. Maldecía la falsedad del ungüento, y quejábase de la credulidad de sus amigos y del poco advertimiento que había tenido en no hacer primero la experiencia en otro, antes de hacerla en Carrizales. En esto llegó la dueña y le aseguró que el viejo dormía a más y mejor. Sosegó el pecho y estuvo atento a muchas palabras amorosas que Marialonso le dijo, de las cuales coligió la mala intención suya, y propuso en sí de ponerla por anzuelo para pescar a su señora. Y estando los dos en sus pláticas, las demás criadas, que estaban escondidas por diversas partes de la casa, una de aquí y otra de allí, volvieron a ver si era verdad que su amo había despertado; y viendo que todo estaba sepultado en silencio, llegaron a la sala donde habían dejado a su señora, de la cual supieron el sueño de su amo; y preguntándole por el músico y por la dueña, les dijo dónde estaban, y todas, con el mismo silencio que habían traído, se llegaron a escuchar por entre las puertas lo que entrambos trataban.

No faltó de la junta Guiomar la negra; el negro sí, porque así como oyó que su amo había despertado, se abrazó con su guitarra y se fue a esconder en su pajar, y cubierto con la manta de su pobre cama sudaba y trasudaba de miedo; y con todo eso no dejaba de tentar las cuerdas de la guitarra, tanta era (encomendado él sea a Satanás) la afición que tenía a la música.

Entreoyeron las mozas los requiebros de la vieja, y cada una le dijo el nombre de las Pascuas:[129]ninguna la llamó vieja que no fuese con su epíteto y adjetivo de hechicera y de barbuda, de antojadiza y de otros que por buen respeto se callan; pero lo que más risa causara a quien entonces las oyera eran las razones de Guiomar la negra, que por ser portuguesa y no muy ladina, era extraña la gracia con que la vituperaba. En efecto, la conclusión de la plática de los dos fue que él condecendería con la voluntad della, cuando ella primero le entregase a toda su voluntad a su señora.

Cuesta arriba se le hizo a la dueña ofrecer lo que el músico pedía; pero a trueco de cumplir el deseo que ya se le había apoderado del alma y de los huesos y médulas del cuerpo, le prometiera los imposibles que pudieran imaginarse. Dejóle y salió a hablar a su señora; y como vio su puerta rodeada de todas las criadas, les dijo que se recogiesen a sus aposentos, que otra noche habría lugar para gozar con menos o con ningún sobresalto del músico, que ya aquella noche el alboroto les había aguado el gusto.

Bien entendieron todas que la vieja se quería quedar sola; pero no pudieron dejar de obedecerla, porque las mandaba a todas. Fuéronse las criadas, y ella acudió a la sala a persuadir a Leonora acudiese a la voluntad de Loaysa, con una larga y tan concertada arenga que pareció que de muchos días la tenía estudiada. Encarecióle su gentileza, su valor, su donaire y sus muchas gracias. Pintóle de cuánto más gusto le serían los abrazos del amante mozo que los del marido viejo, asegurándole el secreto y la duración del deleite con otras cosas semejantes a éstas que el demonio le puso en la lengua, llenas de colores retóricos[130] tan demostrativos y eficaces que movieran no sólo el corazón tierno y poco advertido de la simple e incauta Leonora, sino el de un endurecido mármol. ¡Oh dueñas, nacidas y usadas en el mundo para perdición de mil recatadas y buenas intenciones! ¡Oh luengas y repulgadas tocas,[131] escogidas para autorizar las salas y los estrados de señoras principales! ¡Y cuán al revés de lo que debíades usáis de vuestro casi ya forzoso oficio! En fin, tanto dijo la dueña, tanto persuadió la dueña, que Leonora se rindió, Leonora se engañó y Leonora se perdió, dando en tierra con todas las prevenciones del discreto Carrizales, que dormía el sueño de la muerte de su honra.

Tomó Marialonso por la mano a su señora, y casi por fuerza, preñados de lágrimas los ojos, la llevó donde Loaysa estaba, y echándoles la bendición con una risa falsa de demonio, cerrando tras sí la puerta, los dejó encerrados, y ella se puso a dormir en el estrado o, por mejor decir, a esperar su contento de recudida.[132] Pero como el desvelo de las pasadas noches la venciese, se quedó dormida en el estrado.

Bueno fuera en esta sazón preguntar a Carrizales, a no saber que dormía, que adónde estaban sus advertidos recatos, sus recelos, sus advertimientos, sus persuasiones, los altos muros de su casa, el no haber entrado en ella, ni aun en sombra, alguien que tuviese nombre de varón, el torno estrecho, las gruesas paredes, las ventanas sin luz, el encerramiento notable, la gran dote en que a Leonora había dotado, los regalos continuos que le hacía, el buen tratamiento de sus criadas y esclavas, el no faltar un punto a todo aquello que él imaginaba que habían menester, que podían desear. Pero ya queda dicho que no había para qué preguntárselo, porque dormía más de aquello que fuera menester. Y si él lo oyera y acaso respondiera, no podía dar mejor respuesta que encoger los hombros y enarcar las cejas, y decir: «Todo aqueso derribó por los fundamentos la astucia, a lo que yo creo, de un mozo holgazán y vicioso, y la malicia de una falsa dueña, con la inadvertencia de una muchacha rogada y persuadida.» Libre Dios a cada uno de tales enemigos, contra los cuales no hay escudo de prudencia que defienda ni espada de recato que corte.

Pero, con todo esto, el valor de Leonora fue tal que en el tiempo que más le convenía, lo mostró contra las fuerzas villanas de su astuto engañador, pues no fueron bastantes a vencerla, y él se cansó en balde, y ella quedó vencedora, y entrambos dormidos.

Y en esto ordenó el cielo que a pesar del ungüento, Carrizales despertase; y como tenía de costumbre, tentó la cama por todas partes, y no hallando en ella a su querida esposa, saltó de la cama despavorido y atónito, con más ligereza y denuedo que sus muchos años prometían. Y cuando en el aposento no halló a su esposa y lo vio abierto y que le faltaba la llave de entre los colchones, pensó perder el juicio. Pero, reportándose un poco, salió al corredor, y de allí, andando pie ante pie por no ser sentido, llegó a la sala donde la dueña dormía; y viéndola sola, sin Leonora, fue al aposento de la dueña, y abriendo la puerta muy quedo, vio lo que nunca quisiera haber visto; vio lo que diera por bien empleado no tener ojos para verlo. Vio a Leonora en brazos de Loaysa, durmiendo tan a sueño suelto como si en ellos obrara la virtud del ungüento, y no en el celoso anciano.

Sin pulsos quedó Carrizales con la amarga vista de lo que miraba. La voz se le pegó a la garganta, los brazos se le cayeron de desmayo, y quedó hecho una estatua de mármol frío; y aunque la cólera hizo su natural oficio, avivándole los casi muertos espíritus, pudo tanto el dolor que no le dejó tomar aliento. Y con todo eso tomara la venganza que aquella gran maldad requería, si se hallara con armas para poder tomarla; y así determinó volverse a su aposento a tomar una daga y volver a sacar las manchas de su honra con sangre de sus dos enemigos, y aun con toda aquella de toda la gente de su casa. Con esta determinación honrosa y necesaria volvió, con el mismo silencio y recato que había venido, a su estancia, donde le apretó el corazón tanto el dolor y la angustia que sin ser poderoso a otra cosa, se dejó caer desmayado sobre el lecho.

Llegóse en esto el día, y cogió a los nuevos adúlteros enlazados en la red de sus brazos. Despertó Marialonso, y quiso acudir por lo que a su parecer le tocaba; pero viendo que era tarde, quiso dejarlo para la venidera noche. Alborotóse Leonora viendo tan entrado el día, y maldijo su descuido y el de la maldita dueña, y las dos, con sobresaltados pasos, fueron donde estaba su esposo, rogando entre dientes al cielo que le hallasen todavía roncando; y cuando le vieron encima de la cama callando, creyeron que todavía obraba la untura, pues dormía, y con gran regocijo se abrazaron la una a la otra. Llegóse Leonora a su marido y asiéndole de un brazo, le volvió de un lado a otro por ver si despertaba sin ponerlas en necesidad de lavarle con vinagre, como decían era menester para que en sí volviese. Pero con el movimiento volvió Carrizales de su desmayo, y dando un profundo suspiro, con una voz lamentable y desmayada, dijo:

— ¡Desdichado de mí, y a qué tristes términos me ha traído mi fortuna!

No entendió bien Leonora lo que dijo su esposo; mas como le vio despierto y que hablaba, admirada de ver que la virtud del ungüento no duraba tanto como habían significado, se llegó a él, y poniendo su rostro con el suyo, teniéndole estrechamente abrazado, le dijo:

— ¿Qué tenéis, señor mío, que me parece que os estáis quejando?

Oyó la voz de la dulce enemiga suya el desdichado viejo, y abriendo los ojos desencajadamente, como atónito y embelesado, los puso en ella, y con gran ahínco, sin mover pestaña, la estuvo mirando una gran pieza, al cabo de la cual le dijo:

— Hacedme placer, señora, que luego luego enviéis a llamar a vuestros padres de mi parte, porque siento no sé qué en el corazón, que me da grandísima fatiga, y temo que brevemente me va a quitar la vida, y querríalos ver antes que me muriese.

Sin duda creyó Leonora ser verdad lo que su marido le decía, pensando antes que la fortaleza del ungüento, y no lo que había visto, le tenía en aquel trance; y respondiéndole que haría lo que le mandaba, mandó al negro que luego al punto fuese a llamar a sus padres; y abrazándose con su esposo, le hacía las mayores caricias que jamás le había hecho, preguntándole qué era lo que sentía, con tan tiernas y amorosas palabras como si fuera la cosa del mundo que más amaba. Él la miraba con el embelesamiento que se ha dicho, siéndole cada palabra o caricia que le hacía una lanzada que le atravesaba el alma.

Ya la dueña había dicho a la gente de casa y a Loaysa la enfermedad de su amo, encareciéndoles que debía de ser de momento,[133] pues se le había olvidado de mandar cerrar las puertas de la calle cuando el negro salió a llamar a los padres de su señora; de la cual embajada asimismo se admiraron, por no haber entrado ninguno dellos en aquella casa después que casaron a su hija.

En fin, todos andaban callados y suspensos, no dando en la verdad de la causa de la indisposición de su amo, el cual de rato en rato tan profunda y dolorosamente suspiraba que con cada suspiro parecía arrancársele el alma.

Lloraba Leonora por verle de aquella suerte, y reíase él con una risa de persona que estaba fuera de sí, considerando la falsedad de sus lágrimas.

En esto llegaron los padres de Leonora, y como hallaron la puerta de la calle y la del patio abiertas y la casa sepultada en silencio y sola, quedaron admirados con no pequeño sobresalto. Fueron al aposento de su yerno, y halláronle, como se ha dicho, siempre clavados los ojos en su esposa, a la cual tenía asida de las manos, derramando los dos muchas lágrimas; ella, con no más ocasión de verlas derramar a su esposo; él, por ver cuán fingidamente ella las derramaba.

Así como sus padres entraron, habló Carrizales, y dijo:

— Siéntense aquí vuestras mercedes, y todos los demás dejen desocupado este aposento, y sólo quede la señora Marialonso.

Hiciéronlo así, y quedando solos los cinco, sin esperar que otro hablase, con sosegada voz, limpiándose los ojos, desta manera dijo Carrizales:

— Bien seguro estoy, padres y señores míos, que no será menester traeros testigos para que me creáis una verdad que quiero deciros. Bien se os debe acordar, que no es posible se os haya caído de la memoria, con cuánto amor, con cuán buenas entrañas,[134] hace hoy un año, un mes, cinco días y nueve horas que me entregasteis a vuestra querida hija por legítima mujer mía. También sabéis con cuánta liberalidad la doté, pues fue tal la dote que más de tres de su misma calidad se pudieran casar con opinión de ricas. Asimismo se os debe acordar la diligencia que puse en vestirla y adornarla de todo aquello que ella se acertó a desear y yo alcancé a saber que le convenía. Ni más ni menos habéis visto, señores, cómo, llevado de mi natural condición y temeroso del mal de que, sin duda, he de morir, y experimentado por mi mucha edad en los extraños y varios acaecimientos del mundo, quise guardar esta joya, que yo escogí y vosotros me disteis, con el mayor recato que me fue posible. Alcé las murallas desta casa, quité la vista a las ventanas de la calle, doblé las cerraduras de las puertas, púsele torno, como a monasterio; desterré perpetuamente della todo aquello que sombra o nombre de varón tuviese. Dile criadas y esclavas que la sirviesen; ni les negué a ellas ni a ella cuanto quisieron pedirme. Hícela mi igual, comuniquéle mis más secretos pensamientos, entreguéle toda mi hacienda. Todas éstas eran obras para que, si bien lo considerara, yo viviera seguro de gozar sin sobresalto lo que tanto me había costado, y ella procurara no darme ocasión a que ningún género de temor celoso entrara en mi pensamiento. Mas como no se puede prevenir con diligencia humana el castigo que la voluntad divina quiere dar a los que en ella no ponen del todo en todo sus deseos y esperanzas, no es mucho que yo quede defraudado en las mías; y que yo mismo haya sido el fabricador del veneno que me va quitando la vida. Pero porque veo la suspensión en que todos estáis, colgados de las palabras de mi boca, quiero concluir los largos preámbulos desta plática con deciros en una palabra lo que no es posible decirse en millares dellas. Digo, pues, señores, que todo lo que he dicho y

Cervantes

hecho ha parado en que esta madrugada hallé a ésta, nacida en el mundo para perdición de mi sosiego y fin de mi vida — y esto, señalando a su esposa —, en los brazos de un gallardo mancebo, que en la estancia desta pestífera dueña ahora está encerrado.

Apenas acabó estas últimas palabras Carrizales cuando a Leonora se le cubrió el corazón, y en las mismas rodillas de su marido se cayó desmayada. Perdió la color Marialonso, y a las gargantas de los padres de Leonora se les atravesó un nudo que no les dejaba hablar palabra. Pero prosiguiendo adelante Carrizales, dijo:

— La venganza que pienso tomar desta afrenta no es ni ha de ser de las que ordinariamente suelen tomarse. Pues quiero que, así como yo fui extremado en lo que hice, así sea la venganza que tomaré, tomándola de mí mismo como del más culpado en este delito; que debiera considerar que mal podían estar ni compadecerse en uno los quince años desta muchacha con los casi ochenta míos.[135] Yo fui el que, como el gusano de seda, me fabriqué la casa donde muriese, y a ti no te culpo, ¡oh niña mal aconsejada! — y diciendo esto se inclinó y besó el rostro de la desmayada Leonora —; no te culpo, digo, porque persuasiones de viejas taimadas y requiebros de mozos enamorados fácilmente vencen y triunfan del poco ingenio que los pocos años encierran. Mas por que todo el mundo vea el valor de los quilates de la voluntad y fe con que te quise, en este último trance de mi vida quiero mostrarlo de modo que quede en el mundo por ejemplo, si no de bondad, al menos de simplicidad jamás oída ni vista; y así, quiero que se traiga luego aquí un escribano para hacer de nuevo mi testamento, en el cual mandaré doblar la dote a Leonora y le rogaré que después de mis días, que serán bien breves, disponga su voluntad, pues lo podrá hacer sin fuerza, a casarse con aquel mozo, a quien nunca ofendieron las canas deste lastimado viejo; y así verá que si viviendo jamás salí un punto de lo que pude pensar ser su gusto, en la muerte hago lo mismo, y quiero que lo tenga[136] con el que ella debe de querer tanto. La demás hacienda mandaré a otras obras pías; y a vosotros, señores míos, dejaré con que podáis vivir honradamente lo que de la vida os queda. La venida del escribano sea luego, porque la pasión que tengo me aprieta de manera que a más andar me va acortando los pasos de la vida.

Esto dicho, le sobrevino un terrible desmayo, y se dejó caer tan junto de Leonora que se juntaron los rostros: extraño y triste espectáculo para los padres que a su querida hija y a su amado yerno miraban. No quiso la mala dueña esperar a las reprehensiones que pensó le darían los padres de su señora; y así se salió del aposento y fue a decir a Loaysa todo lo que pasaba, aconsejándole que luego al punto se fuese de aquella casa, que ella tendría cuidado de avisarle con el negro lo que sucediese, pues ya no había puertas ni llaves que lo impidiesen. Admiróse Loaysa con tales nuevas, y tomando

44

el consejo volvió a vestirse como pobre, y fuese a dar cuenta a sus amigos del extraño y nunca visto suceso de sus amores.

En tanto, pues, que los dos estaban transportados,[137] el padre de Leonora envió a llamar a un escribano amigo suyo, el cual vino a tiempo que ya habían vuelto hija y yerno en su acuerdo. Hizo Carrizales su testamento en la manera que había dicho, sin declarar el yerro de Leonora, más de que por buenos respetos le pedía y rogaba se casase, si acaso él muriese, con aquel mancebo que él le había dicho en secreto. Cuando esto oyó Leonora, se arrojó a los pies de su marido, y saltándole el corazón en el pecho, le dijo:

— Vivid vos muchos años, mi señor y mi bien todo, que puesto caso que no estáis obligado a creerme ninguna cosa de las que os dijere, sabed que no os he ofendido sino con el pensamiento.

Y comenzando a disculparse y a contar por extenso la verdad del caso, no pudo mover la lengua, y volvió a desmayarse. Abrazóla así desmayada el lastimado viejo; abrazáronla sus padres; lloraron todos tan amargamente que obligaron y aun forzaron a que en ellas les acompañase el escribano que hacía el testamento, en el cual dejó de comer a todas las criadas de casa, horras las esclavas y el negro,[138] y a la falsa de Marialonso no le mandó otra cosa que la paga de su salario; mas sea lo que fuere, el dolor le apretó de manera que al seteno día le llevaron a la sepultura.

Quedó Leonora viuda, llorosa y rica; y cuando Loaysa esperaba que cumpliese lo que ya él sabía que su marido en su testamento dejaba mandado, vio que dentro de una semana se entró monja en uno de los más recogidos monasterios de la ciudad. Él, despechado y casi corrido,[139] se pasó a las Indias. Quedaron los padres de Leonora tristísimos, aunque se consolaron con lo que su yerno les había dejado y mandado por su testamento. Las criadas se consolaron con lo mismo, y las esclavas y esclavo con la libertad; y la malvada de la dueña, pobre y defraudada de todos sus malos pensamientos.

Y yo quedé con el deseo de llegar al fin deste suceso, ejemplo y espejo de lo poco que hay que fiar de llaves, tornos y paredes cuando queda la voluntad libre; y de lo menos que hay que confiar de verdes y pocos años, si les andan al oído exhortaciones destas dueñas de monjil negro y tendido y tocas blancas y luengas.[140] Sólo no sé qué fue la causa que Leonora no puso más ahínco en disculparse y dar a entender a su celoso marido cuán limpia y sin ofensa había quedado en aquel suceso; pero la turbación le ató la lengua, y la prisa que se dio a morir su marido no dio lugar a su disculpa.

45

NOTES TO *EL CELOSO EXTREMEÑO*

1. un hidalgo, nacido de padres nobles: *hidalgo*: 'nobleman'; usually, as here, a member of the lower or petty nobility. More wealthy men could buy *hidalguía* subject to certain conditions, but Carrizales' nobility is inherited. Inherited nobility was regarded as superior to bought nobility, or was by those who possessed it. In the census of 1541 the percentage of nobles in the population ranged from 7% to 50% depending on the province. Northern Spain had larger proportions than the south.

2. un otro Pródigo: A reference to the Prodigal Son (*Luke* 15: 11-32).

3. Italia y Flandes: In the second half of the sixteenth century Flanders, the Kingdom of Naples, and other parts of Italy belonged to the Spanish empire.

4. iglesia de los alzados: 'sanctuary of the bankrupt'. 'Alzarse el banco es quebrar de su crédito' (Covarrubias, under *alçar*).

5. pala y cubierta de los jugadores a quien llaman *ciertos* los peritos en el arte: *cierto*: the member of a team of card-sharps who supplied the trick cards. He was assisted by the *enganchador*, whose task was to lure ('hook': *enganchar*) the players to be duped; and by the *rufián*, whose task was that of hiding the cards as soon as the game had finished (Néstor Luján, *La vida cotidiana en el Siglo de Oro español*, 5th ed. [Barcelona: Planeta, 1989], p. 166). *Peritos*: 'experts' or 'professionals' in the art of cheating at cards. Like *cierto*, *enganchador*, and *rufián* (in the card-playing context), *pala* and *cubierta* are from the criminal slang that was known as *germanía*. Freely translatable as 'cover' and 'hide-out', they refer to forms of trickery. 'Hacer pala....ponerse un ladrón delante de alguno a quien quieren robar, para ocultarle la vista' (*Dic. Aut.*, under *pala*). *Cubierta*: 'simulación o artificio con que se oculta alguna cosa, haciéndola parecer diferente' (ibid., under *cubierta*). The introduction of *germanía* adds interest to Cervantes' narrative and is an economical way of creating lifelike atmosphere. He was fond of enriching the curiosity value and verisimilitude of his own works with his knowledge of places, social types and social customs with which few or none of his readers would have been familar; but his information is not always reliable.

6. llegado el tiempo en que una flota se partía para Tierra Firme, acomodándose con el almirante della: *Tierra Firme*: the Caribbean region of lower central America (excluding the islands) and continental south

America. The whole area (including the islands) was known as the 'Spanish Main' in contemporary England. Transatlantic shipping was organised in fleets for greater protection against piracy and hostile warships. By law of 1564 there were two annual sailings, one to Nueva España (Mexico) in the month of April and the second to Tierra Firme in the month of August, though these schedules were often missed. See Hamilton, p. 19. The fleet commanders were captains general, not admirals as Cervantes calls them, and passengers would normally have dealt with the masters of individual ships and not with the fleet commander.

7. mortaja de esparto: An esparto mat for sleeping on; used by poorer passengers. Literally an 'esparto shroud'.

8. el mar Océano: 'the Ocean' or 'Ocean Sea'. 'Llamamos [océano] al mar que cerca toda la tierra....toma nombres particulares, como Atlántico' (Covarrubias, under *océano*). The name derives from Greek cosmography.

9. Felipo de Carrizales: In the first edition the forms *Felipo* and *Filipo* both occur. *Felipo* and *Filipo* are more Classical versions of *Felipe*, a name evolved from the Greek name *Philippos*. Both are found as versions of *Felipe II*: King Philip II. *Carrizales* is an authentic name but a very unusual one. It befits the character's individuality (the extremeness of his jealousy) and makes him more memorable. It may also be a characternym (a name that actually describes the character in some way). A *carrizal* is the place where *carrizos* grow. A *carrizo* is a tough and spiny reed in Covarrubias' definition of the word.

10. Cartagena: Cartagena de Indias was the major port in the administrative region of Nueva Granada, roughly equivalent to modern Colombia, in the viceroyalty of Peru. Called *el Pirú* in Cervantes' day, viceregal Peru was much larger than the modern republic.

11. ciento y cincuenta mil pesos ensayados: '150,000 assayed *pesos* [of silver and gold]'. *Peso*: a unit of account for bullion, probably equivalent to 450 *maravedís*. The *maravedí* was a unit of account of wider application and was equivalent until 1602 to 0·094 grams of silver [Hamilton, p. 318]. Most of the treasure imported in the later sixteenth century was silver. Combined imports of gold and silver peaked in 1591-5 (ibid., p. 35). Carrizales' fortune amounts to approximately 0.4% of the registered imports of treasure for this period (about 35 million *pesos* [loc. cit.]) and he is easily the equivalent of a modern millionaire (sterling millionaire) several times over. To give an idea of his relative worth, about 270 *maravedís* was a daily wage for an Andalusian master mason in 1601 (ibid., p. 400).

12. trayéndola toda en barras de oro y plata, y registrada, por quitar inconvenientes, se volvió a España. Desembarcó en Sanlúcar; llegó a Sevilla... sacó sus partidas sin zozobras: These words refer in skeletal form to a regulated procedure that is described in detail by Hamilton (ch. 2). Passengers from the

Indies were legally required to register treasure (gold and silver) with an official called the *maestre de plata* who accompanied the fleet and who was responsible for ensuring that all treasure was conveyed to the Casa de la Contratación in Seville. Seville was the required destination of fleets returning from the Indies. The Casa de la Contratación (House of Trade) was the government body in supervisory charge of transatlantic shipping and trade. Ships put in at Sanlúcar de Barrameda. There no one was permitted to disembark before an official from the House of Trade had carried out an inspection. One of his tasks was to open chests in search of unregistered treasure. (One way of smuggling treasure was to transfer it to smaller craft before arrival in Sanlúcar or before the inspector had arrived, but the authorities were alert to this ruse and regulations existed to foil it.) The treasure was then taken to the House of Trade for weighing and storing until the nearby Consejo de Indias, the Council which supervised the House of Trade, authorised the *maestre de plata* to release it. Those who successfully smuggled evaded taxes and the requirement that treasure should be delivered to a mint for conversion into coins, but unregistered treasure was confiscated if it was found. Carrizales obeyed the regulations to avoid complications and the risk of being discovered. Like most old men, he no longer had the stomach for stressful living. **sacó sus partidas sin zozobras:** 'he collected his property without running into trouble'. The word *zozobra* literally denoted a strong headwind that made a ship's passage bumpy. Covarrubias compares the effect to sailing over stones (under *çoçobra*).

13. continuo: *continuadamente, siempre.*

14. no por miserable: 'not out of miserliness'.

15. tenerlas en ser era cosa infructuosa: 'it was unprofitable to keep them as they were', i.e. to make no use of them. Cervantes seems to be ignorant here in the light of modern research. Most private treasure was sold to merchants and the law required treasure to be coined (n. 12). Owners could not take possession of it from the *maestre de plata* until they had officially accepted this obligation (Hamilton, p. 29).

16. al inquieto trato de las mercancías: Even if we are meant to understand by this that Carrizales had traded in precious metals rather than in other commodities or in manufactured goods, *el trato de las mercancías* is a strange background to give him, considering that he possessed no capital when he emigrated to the Indies. From an economic point of view a more plausible background would have been prospecting and mining. Cervantes perhaps rejected this option in the light of Carrizales' nobility. Physical work was for commoners, in the traditional opinion of *hidalgos*.

17. dar en ella su hacienda a tributo: 'earn interest [there] on his estate' (Thacker). The *tierra* is his native region, Extremadura, in the Kingdom of Castile.

18. la estrecheza de su patria era mucha y la gente muy pobre: Extremadura has always been one of the poorer parts of Spain.

19. a lo que muestra la presencia desta casa: 'judging by the appearance of this house'.

20. Casarme he: *Me casaré.*

21. haréla a mis mañas: 'I'll make her my creature'. *Maña* implies scheming.

22. para todos: *para todos los casos.*

23. supo como: 'discovered that'; *como = que.* This usage occurs elsewhere.

24. habiéndola dotado primero en veinte mil ducados: It was customary for a wife to contribute resources to a marriage in the form of a dowry (*dote*), which would normally be supplied by her parents. Dowries consisted of money and/or other assets and formed part of the wife's estate. A contemporary reader would have known very well that Leonora is disadvantaged by her parents' poverty and requires a husband for whom dowries do not matter. The dowry supplied by Carrizales guarantees her financial security. A ducat was a unit of account with a value of 375 *maravedís* (Hamilton, p. 55n) and 20,000 ducats was probably the equivalent of more than twice a lifetime's income for most people. The arrangement made by Carrizales is an extraordinary adaptation of the custom of paying *arras*. The *arras* were a sum of money that the future groom or the groom's parents, in the case of a dependent son, would normally pay at the time of the betrothal as a sign of good faith. The *arras* would be held by the bride's parents until the marriage took place and would then form part of the groom's contribution to matrimonial funds. If the bride was jilted, her parents could keep the money.

25. una saya de raja y una ropilla de tafetán: *saya:* 'skirt'; *raja:* a cheap cloth, '*quasi* rasa, porque no le queda pelo como a los demás paños' (Covarrubias); *una ropilla de tafetán:* 'a top made from taffeta'. A *ropilla* was an upper garment worn over a bodice.

26. agua de pie: running water (*Dic. Aut.*, under *agua de pie*), probably from a stonework *fuente*.

27. portal de la calle: 'front entrance', from the street.

28. tapicerías, estrados y doseles: Furnishings associated with the highest social classes. An *estrado* was a low, rug-covered platform where ladies sat on cushions, Moorish-style, to talk and receive visitors. It was also the platform on which monarchs sat at public events, or the stateroom in which royal officials held audiences (see Covarrubias, under *estrado* and *estrados*). A *dosel* was a canopy suspended above a dining-table; a furnishing that Covarrubias associates with monarchs, the high nobility and prelates (under *dosel*).

29. cuatro esclavas blancas, y herrólas en el rostro, y otras dos negras bozales: White slaves: probably lighter-skinned North Africans, possibly

Cervantes

Turks or *moriscos* (descendants of the Spanish Moors). **herrólas en el rostro:** The facial branding of slaves was normal practice. **bozales:** See Glossary. The majority of black slaves originated in Portuguese Africa. The one *bozal* who is named and who speaks, Guiomar, is described as 'portuguesa' (p. 212). Slavery was more characteristic of the south of Spain and the largest slave population was in Seville. The number of slaves in Seville in the early seventeenth century has been estimated at over six thousand.

30. un despensero que le trajese y comprase de comer: A *despensero* was normally a 'steward' in charge of the larder and sometimes other supplies in a wealthy home (Covarrubias, under *despender*). This *despensero* is an external 'victualler'.

31. dio parte de su hacienda a censo, situada en diversas y buenas partes: He used part of his wealth as a financier, funding property purchases in a diversity of good locations and receiving his remuneration in the form of mortgages or annuities:

> Censo. Cerca de los romanos era la renta, tributo o entrada que cada uno tenía según el valor de su hacienda; de modo que censo significaba la hacienda y también la renta que por ella le daban... Comúnmente llamamos censo el que tenemos cargado sobre algunos bienes raíces; y éste suele ser al quitar que estará en voluntad del censatario que lo paga dar el principal y redimirlo....censo de por vida, que se da como pensión por los días que tal persona viviere, pocos o muchos. Y entonces el uno y el otro se ponen a su aventura.
>
> (Covarrubias)

32. para lo que se le ofreciese: 'for whatever opportunities might arise'.

33. los días de fiesta: 'holy days'. Sundays and other days when the Church required attendance at Mass, called 'días de obligación' in the early text of the novella.

34. dieron en ser golosas: A form of gluttony, and for a contemporary reader probably an omen of lust. A sweet tooth in women was proverbially associated with sexual corruption and crime. For example: 'La mujer golosa, o puta o ladrona' (Correas, p. 206a).

35. llaneza de su condición: *condición*: 'disposition'. *Llaneza*: 'straight-forwardness'; simplicity of mind and manner.

36. sólo se desvelaba en traer regalos a su esposa y en acordarle le pidiese todos cuantos le viniesen al pensamiento: This is later contradicted: 'De día pensaba, de noche no dormía; él era la ronda y centinela de su casa y el Argos de lo que bien quería' (p. 23).

37. de condición llana: Like his wife. See n. 35.

38. pasaron un año de noviciado e hicieron profesión en aquella vida:

50

An ironical comparison with novice nuns taking their final vows of poverty, chastity and obedience. The phrase *hacer profesión* is straight from the language of convents.

39. el sagaz perturbador del género humano: Satan.

40. monasterio: Both 'monastery' and 'convent' were normal meanings of the term.

41. manzanas de oro tan guardadas: A witty Classical allusion and a good example of the economy of Cervantes' art. The Golden Apples were given by Gaia (Earth) to Hera when she married Zeus. They grew in the Garden of the Hesperides (Daughters of the Night) and were protected by a monster called Ladon. One of the Twelve Labours of Hercules was to capture them from the monster. Cervantes implicitly compares Carrizales to Ladon, and Loaysa (the interloper to whom the rest of the sentence alludes) to Hercules. The tale is momentarily viewed as a sordid 'real-life' version of the Herculean myth, or as a distant parody of that myth.

42. hijos de vecino de cada colación: 'sons of all the local clans'. 'Colación algunas veces significa los vecinos que son de una misma parroquia o tribu' (Covarrubias).

43. gente baldía, atildada y meliflua: 'idle, affected, smooth-talking people'.

44. *virote* (mozo soltero; que a los recién casados llaman *mantones*): *virote*: slang use of a word that had various formal meanings. In this context it literally denotes a type of crossbow bolt, according to the early text:

> a los mozos solteros llaman también *virotes*, porque así como los virotes se disparan a muchas partes, éstos no tienen asiento ninguno en ninguna, y andan vagando de barrio en barrio.
>
> (ed. Avalle-Arce, p. 233)

mantones: The meaning of this word is different in the early text, where *mantones* are described as certain 'viejos ancianos y hombres maduros' (loc. cit.).

45. habiendo entrado en bureo muchas veces: 'having held many business meetings'. The word *bureo* literally denoted 'la junta de los mayordomos [majordomos: housekeeping managers] de la casa real' (Covarrubias).

46. se ponía cada noche a la oración a la puerta de la casa de Carrizales: He may have been saying prayers for passers-by who paid him money to do so. Praying in return for alms was one of the ways in which beggars acquired their money.

47. romances de moros y moras a la loquesca: *romances*: ballads, medieval in origin. Here Moorish ballads (ballads with Moorish characters). The phrase *a la loquesca* (*a lo loco*) probably refers to an energetic style in which ballads were sometimes sung (Rodríguez Marín, p. 109n).

48. hablando con nadie: *hablando con alguien.*

51

49. pidiendo por Dios a la buena gente: He uses the words 'por Dios' or 'por amor de Dios' to appeal for Christian compassion. This is the origin of the word *pordiosero*.

50. morenos: 'coloureds', 'blacks'.

51. veinticuatros: 'aldermen', called *veinticuatros* in some parts of Andalusia. Elsewhere called *regidores*.

52. *La estrella de Venus* **y la de** *Por un verde prado*: *La estrella de Venus* is a Moorish ballad that was very popular in the late sixteenth century and which Lope de Vega probably wrote or perfected. It is ballad no. 33 in *Romancero general o colección de romances castellanos anteriores al siglo XVIII*, ed. Agustín Durán, Biblioteca de Autores Españoles, XII and XVI (Madrid: Sucesores de Hernando, 1924 and 1921), XII. *Por un verde prado*, whose second line is 'salió mi pastora', was perhaps a type of madrigal. Avalle-Arce (p. 187n) found a reference to it as an example of madrigals in Miguel Sánchez's *El arte poética en romance castellano* [*The Art of Poetry in Castilian*], published in 1580. Like 'Madre, la mi madre,/guardas me ponéis', the brief references to popular songs are attuned to the novella's subject-matter. *Por un verde prado* evokes an idealised natural world (a pastoral world) which contrasts with that of *El celoso extremeño* and highlights its overlapping motifs of artifice, bondage and perversion. *La estrella de Venus* is a harmonic text that stresses the power of money. Gazul's beloved agrees to marry another man, Albenzaide, whose only attraction is his wealth (he is described as 'feo y torpe'). Gazul intervenes and kills him. The introduction of popular songs that mirror or sharpen the themes of the work is characteristic of *comedias. El celoso extremeño* is unusual by dramatic standards in introducing a series of songs through fragments or mere references which the reader is required to expand.

53. A los hierros de una reja/la turbada mano asida: The beginning of a Moorish ballad: no. 107 in *Romancero de Barcelona,* ed. R. Foulché-Delbosc, *Revue Hispanique,* 29 (1913), 121-94. Though the quoted fragment is attuned to the novella's theme of bondage, the rest of the ballad is more closely related to the theme of *engaño* and particularly to the subject of a false accusation levelled against a woman. Its heroine, Zaida, is a victim of spiteful lies.

54. Abindarráez...Jarifa: Characters in Moorish ballads in which jealousy is an important motif: nos. 75-84 in *Romancero general o colección de romances castellanos anteriores al siglo XVIII*, ed. Agustín Durán, *Biblioteca de autores españoles,* X (Madrid: Librería de los Sucesores de Hernando, 1924).

55. las...de la historia del gran Sofí Tomunibeyo, con las de la zarabanda a lo divino: *Tomunibeyo*, which is perhaps a misprinting of *Tomumbeyo*, is probably a reference to Tumanbai II (Ashraf Tumanbai), who was the last of the Mameluke sultans of Egypt (1516-17). He resisted the invasion by the Ottoman Sultan, or Grand Turk, Selim I, and was captured and executed. No one has discovered Spanish songs about either him or his predecessor (Tumanbai I) and unless Cervantes is more ignorant here than he usually is about the Muslim world, 'gran Sofí Tomunibeyo' is a deliberate confusion of Egyptian sultans with shahs. 'Sufí' was not an Egyptian title but one that was used by the Safawid shahs of Persia (1499-1736). It is possible that *gran* should be *Gran*. This would introduce a further confusion with the rulers of the Ottoman Empire (the Grand Turks). The joke mocks Luis's ignorance and gullibility, but it is also an instance of one-upmanship over readers, for few of them would have possessed enough knowledge of the Muslim world to appreciate the ethnic confusion. Most of them would probably have thought that Loaysa was inventing songs about a shah. It seems safe to assume that the reference to *zarabandas a lo divino* is another joke of a more accessible kind. In this case, Luis's failure to appreciate the joke convicts him of plain obtuseness. The description *a lo divino* was given to poetic and lyrical works of a secular nature that had been rewritten on Christian lines. The *zarabanda* was a popular song and dance. No one has discovered *zarabandas a lo divino* and they sound like an impossibility. The danced *zarabanda* was notorious for its indecency (see n. 85), so a pious *zarabanda* would probably have lost its crucial component, the dance, or have been unrecognisable as a *zarabanda*. Loaysa's complacency in duping Luis and the latter's unfailing stupidity are very reminiscent of the mechanical humour of the trickster/*bobo* relationship in *entremeses*, where the dupe infallibly disgraces himself and is confidently expected to do so.

56. hacen pasmar a los mismos portugueses: The Portuguese were renowned in Spain for their lyricism and sentimentality.

57. apenas habréis comido tres o cuatro moyos de sal, cuando ya os veáis músico corriente y moliente en todo género de guitarra: *músico corriente y moliente*: 'a regular maestro'. 'Moliente y corriente. Del molino que está cumplido en todo lo que ha menester, y por metáfora se dice de cualquier otra cosa' (Covarrubias, under *moliente*). **tres o cuatro moyos de sal:** A *moyo* was a large amount. As a liquid measure its approximate range was 250 to 260 litres (Hamilton, p. 171) and as a dry measure its range was probably the same. Covarrubias speaks of *moyos* as heaps of grain arranged on threshing floors (under *mojón*). Loaysa is having a private joke, exploiting Luis's ignorance or obtuseness.

58. guardas: 'wards': the indentations in the key.

59. preste Juan de las Indias: Prester John was a mythical Christian king and priest who according to medieval legend ruled over vast territories somewhere in the 'Indies' (India and adjacent regions) or Africa. From the fourteenth century he was normally associated with Africa, particularly Abyssinia; but the title 'Prester John of the Indies' stuck. The idea of him taking guitar tutorials from a crippled Spanish beggar – and just the idea of an exotic figure called *preste Juan de las Indias* taking guitar lessons – is clearly a form of bathos.

60. ora sea de guitarra o clavicímbano: *ora sea = ahora sea. Clavicímbano*: similar to a clavichord; called *clavicímbalo* by Covarrubias (under *clavicordio*). Socially an upper-class instrument, in contrast to the guitar.

61. con la misma: *con la misma facilidad.*

62. con aprovechamiento de mi persona y aumento de vuestra suficiencia: 'to my benefit and the betterment of your skills'.

63. relieves: 'leftovers'.

64. puesto que: *aunque* ('even if').

65. Pues a la mano de Dios: 'To work, then'. The Spanish expression is ironic, in view of the ungodly nature of Loaysa's purpose. The irony is probably author's irony rather than the character's private joke, given the idiomatic nature of the expression.

66. cosas flemosas: A reference to the contemporary theory of body chemistry known as the Four Humours: blood, yellow bile, black bile, and phlegm. Luis is told to keep off foods that increase the level of phlegm.

67. el suelo: The sense must be 'earth' or 'world'.

68. azumbre: A liquid measure roughly equivalent to two litres (Hamilton, p. 171).

69. botilla, que también cabe justas dos azumbres: The diminutive *-illa* is comic, in view of the capacity of this particular *bota* (wineskin).

70. que según yo os enseñare, así me pagaréis: 'pay me as well as I teach you'; or 'If I teach you well you can pay me accordingly' (Thacker). I have preferred *enseñare*, future subjunctive, to the indicative *enseñaré*.

71. Sea en buena hora: 'Let's hope so' (Thacker).

72. romancito agudo: As used here *agudo* is a prosodic term. *Romances* (ballads) rhyme in either single or double assonance. In a *romance agudo* the rhyme is single and based upon the final syllable of words in which this syllable carries the word-stress, e.g. *señor, habló, afición*. These are *palabras agudas*. A word in which the penultimate syllable carries the stress is prosodically known as *llana* ('plain', 'flat'). Most Spanish words are *llanas*.

73. a no ser mirado con malicia y sospechosamente no se podía caer en el agujero: *caer* in the sense of *caer en la cuenta*; 'only a crafty and suspicious eye would have been able to tell that it was there' (Thacker).

74. Orfeo: A Classical allusion with hidden elements of wit, comparable therefore to the reference to the Golden Apples (n. 41). Orpheus was a mythical poet and musician who played the lyre, a sublime instrument in the poetic culture of the Renaissance and seventeenth century. He was also the husband of Euridice. When Euridice was killed by a snake, Orpheus descended into Hades in order to rescue her. Euridice was released from Hades on condition that Orpheus did not look back till he reached the upper world, but he did look back at the last moment and Euridice was taken away. Loaysa is a parodic version both of the Orpheus who played the lyre (Loaysa plays the guitar: a plebeian instrument, associated with streets and taverns) and of the Orpheus who descended into Hades: his aims in penetrating Carrizales' house strike an ironical moral contrast with those of the Classical hero. The allusion is also a dark foreshadowing of the novella's ironic ending. Leonora's eleventh-hour resilience and her decision not to marry Loaysa but to shut herself away in a convent distantly evoke the Classical hero's loss of Euridice.

75. todos aquellos que no fueren industriosos y tracistas morirán de hambre: *tracista* here means a person who uses cunning; 'anyone who isn't resourceful and cunning will starve to death'.

76. En buen hora: 'Fine, let's do it'.

77. torzal de cera: A kind of 'wax taper': waxed and twisted cord.

78. aunque con dulce: 'although the music was sweet' (Thacker) seems less likely than 'although the food was sweet'.

79. como el pobre negro tenía cuatro dedos de vino sobre los sesos, no acertaba traste: 'since the poor black man was pickled in wine, he got all the frets wrong'.

80. a obra de: 'at about'.

81. luego: 'right now'.

82. clausura: A monastic image: 'Clausura. El encerramiento de algún lugar religioso o monasterio' (Covarrubias); 'monastic confinement'.

83. en su casa le faltara: Concealed hunger is a common theme in contemporary literature and is usually associated with impoverished *hidalgos*. Cervantes' remark seems careless, however, since the *gente de barrio* are idle sons of the rich (p. 24).

84. cecear: To make a kind of hissing sound in order to catch someone's attention (like English 'psst') or to demand someone's silence (like 'shsh').

85. ¿qué diré de lo que ellas sintieron cuando le oyeron tocar el *Pésame dello* y acabar con el endemoniado son de la zarabanda, nuevo entonces en España?: The *zarabanda* and the *Pésame dello* were two of a number of *bailes cantados* that women danced and whose dancing style had a reputation for lewdness. Both are described as diabolical in Cervantes' *entremés*, *La cueva de Salamanca*. He probably felt that their critics were oversensitive (the *entremés* condemnation is a humorous one) but he evidently understood their feelings and shared them in some degree. The *zarabanda* appears to have been the most scandalous dance of the period. Clerical observers of public morals attempted to have it banned. Note the proverb: 'A la mujer bailar y al asno rebuznar, el diablo se lo debió de mostrar' (Covarrubias, under *baylar*).

86. coplillas de la seguida: *seguida*: a type of popular song and dance; also called *seguidas, seguidilla* or *seguidillas. Coplas*: the verses of a popular song, and sometimes the refrain in particular.

87. con tan buenas razones que ellas echaron de ver: 'so eloquently that they fully realised'.

88. polvos de vida para todas nosotras: Note that Carrizales' house has already been compared to a tomb: 'les pareció que la llevaban a la sepultura' (p. 22).

89. quedando de: *quedando en*: 'agreeing to'.

90. un cruzado: A simple three-finger position on the fingerboard of the guitar, producing the chord D major.

91. sin haberle visto, le alababa [Marialonso] y le subía sobre Absalón y sobre Orfeo: Absalom was the most handsome man in Israel (II *Samuel* 14: 25). On Orpheus, see n. 74. The praise is both passionate and self-serving. Leonora must be won over if the relationship with Loaysa is to progress.

92. hubo de hacer: 'was forced to do' (Thacker), 'could not help doing'.

93. calzones grandes de tafetán leonado, anchos a la marineresca, un jubón de lo mismo con trencillas de oro, y una montera de raso de la misma color, con cuello almidonado con grandes puntas y encaje: 'generous breeches of tawny-coloured taffeta, in the wide sailor's style, a gold-braided doublet made out of the same material, a satin hunting-cap of the same colour, and a starched ruff with large lace frills'. In general a dandified appearance. The breeches are later described as *gregüescos* (p. 36), which Don Quixote says, in one of his lucid and *discreto* moments, a gentleman should never wear (*Don Quijote* II.43).

94. por brújula: *brújula*: the small hole in a sighting device, e.g. the sights of an astrolabe or harquebus. The phrase *por brújula* is a card-playing metaphor. It refers to the skill of identifying a card by scrutinising its border. 'Los jugadores de naipes que muy de espacio van descubriendo las cartas, y por sola la raya antes que pinte el naipe discurren la que puede ser, dicen que miran por brújula y que brujulean' (Covarrubias, under *brúxula*).

95. con muchas veras: 'with great earnestness'.

96. honra: See *El viejo celoso*, n. 13.

97. El Rey tiene harta: A proverbial expression of disdain for honour, virtually meaning 'Leave honour to the King'.

98. Matusalén: The biblical figure Methuselah who lived for 969 years (*Genesis* 5: 27).

99. clausura: See n. 82.

100. perro que salta por el Rey de Francia: 'Salta por el Rey de Francia' was a command used by blind beggars to make their dogs do tricks: '«Salta por el Rey de Francia», y [el perro] salta; «Salta por la mala tabernera», y no salta' (Correas, p. 583b).

101. y besalla que lo veamos todas: 'and kiss it for all to see'.

102. con mi boca sucia: A phrase that occurs in other works of this period and was probably often used in swearing oaths. It may be a form of 'dramatic' irony (author's irony) but is unlikely to be a private joke in the mind of the speaker, Loaysa.

103. el *tuáutem* de todo: 'the key thing'. A *tuáutem* is 'el sujeto que se tiene por principal y necesario para alguna cosa o la cosa misma que se considera precisa. Es compuesto de las voces latinas *tu* y *autem*' (*Dic. Aut.*).

104. puesto que: *aunque* ('although').

105. el término que quiere: *el término que el pensamiento quiere.*

106. velado: 'Velo. El que lleva la novia cuando se casa, de donde se llamó aquel acto velambres y ella [bride] y él [groom] velado y velada' (Covarrubias). Cervantes is reporting Leonora's own words and her use of *velado* may seem ambivalent in an unwitting and ironic way (an instance of 'dramatic' or author's irony). If associated with the verb *velar* in the sense of 'to stay awake' in order to keep vigil, it alludes to her husband's jealousy.

107. luego luego: 'straightaway'.

108. alopiado ungüento: *alopiado* is an Italianism (from *alloppiato*) for *opiado*; 'doped' or 'drugged ointment'.

109. más ha de una hora: *hace más de una hora.*

110. la alzaron en peso como a catedrático: A reference to the custom of chair-lifting victors in competitions for professorships.

111. ¡Ea, pues, amiga!: 'Come on, then, sister!'

112. ¡démonos un verde de música que no haya más que ver!: 'Darse un verde, holgarse en banquetes y placeres' (Covarrubias, under *verde*).

113. le hemos de tomar juramento, como la otra noche: It was Leonora who demanded an oath on the previous night and here Marialonso is carrying out her mistress's orders that the oath should be repeated. Marialonso's support of her mistress is a tactical necessity (Leonora will not let Loaysa in unless he swears an oath) but her orders are no burden for her, since all that her mistress now demands of Loaysa is that he accept the women's authority. The demand implies an innocent kind of complacency. Leonora fears the lesser danger (an uncontrolled Loaysa) and ignores the greater danger (her own sexuality and that of her female companions).

114. mal pecado: An expression of regret, like '¡qué desgracia!'. It could be either an indiscretion on the *dueña*'s part or a shameless signal that she regards her chastity as a social imposition.

115. corrimientos: 'Corrido, el confuso y afrentado. Corrimiento, la tal confusión y vergüenza. Andar corrido, andar o afrentado o trabajado de una parte a otra' (Covarrubias, under *correr*). The meaning is seemingly 'rushing around', in the harassed sense of 'trabajado de una parte a otra'.

116. **Por mí, más que nunca jura, entre con todo diablo; que aunque más jura, si acá estás, todo olvida:** 'Ever much he swear, me think he still come in with devil. Though he swear more, if you are here, he forget everything.'

117. **una obligación guarentigia:** 'a binding obligation' (Thacker). *Guarentigia* is a legal term, an Italianism, and a word that Loaysa uses in order to impress (he is about to declare that his rough exterior disguises refinement and learning). It is unlikely that his audience understands it. 'Aplicábase al contrato, escritura [deed, document] o cláusula de ella en que se daba poder a las justicias para que la hiciesen cumplir' (Real Academia Española, *Diccionario de la lengua española*, 21st edition, 2 vols [Madrid: RAE, 1992]).

118. **debajo del sayal hay ál, y que debajo de mala capa suele estar un buen bebedor:** Two proverbs with similar senses. The first means that a noble or refined person is hidden beneath a rough exterior. The *ál* means 'otra cosa', from Latin *aliud*. *Sayal*: rough woollen cloth. Covarrubias says of the second proverb: 'Suelen algunos hombres humildes y no conocidos ser de más letras [more learned] y capacidad que los que están en grandes lugares con opinión de muy letrados' (under *capa*).

119. **por la intemerata eficacia, donde más santa y largamente se contiene:** 'by the intemerate [immaculate] efficacy, where it is most sacredly and extensively contained'. A parody of religious discourse and probably of learned prayer to the Virgin. *Intemerata* is from Latin and Italian, though it may not have been all that rare a term in learned religious Spanish. As used here, it may be intended as an amusingly ambivalent term for cognoscenti of Italian. In Italian it could be used as a noun whose meanings included 'muddle' and 'intrigue'. *Eficacia* is a word associated with grace, as in 'efficacious grace', and *donde más santa y largamente se contiene* is probably a reference to Christ (the child in Mary's womb) which parodically muddles religious discourse with a contemporary legal formula: *donde más largamente se contiene*. See Marcel Bataillon, 'Glanes cervantines', *Quaderni Ibero-Americani*, 2 (1953), 393-7 (395-7) and Leo Spitzer, 'Y así juro por la intemerata eficacia...', *Quaderni Ibero-Americani*, 2 (1954), 483-4. Loaysa employs a legal or notarial style in bringing his oath to an end ('desde ahora para entonces...valedero').

120. **por las entradas y salidas del santo Líbano monte:** Another hollow and derisive assurance (though Mount Lebanon is a real place) in which *entradas y salidas* can mean 'entrances and exits', 'income and outgoings', or 'tariffs': 'A la entrada y a la salida: cuando se responde con algún derecho entrando y saliendo en cierto lugar' (Covarrubias, under *entrada*).

121. la verdadera historia de Carlomagno, con la muerte del gigante Fierabrás: Another comic ingredient in the oath, lumping together a historical figure – Charlemagne, the first Holy Roman Emperor – and a fictitious pagan figure, the giant Fierabrás, and alluding to the mendacious world that chivalresque romances constructed around the Emperor. It is probably inspired by one particular work: the *Historia del emperador Carlomagno y de los doce Pares de Francia* (first published in 1521), translated from the French *Fierabras* or *Conqueste du grant Roy Charlemaigne des Espaignes* (Schevill and Bonilla, p. 385n). Fierabrás is mentioned in *Don Quijote* (I.10, 17, 49).

122. sima de Cabra: A subterranean chasm near the town of Cabra in the province of Córdoba. Mentioned in *Don Quijote* II. 14. The speaker may or may not be the maid who echoed the *dueña* in demanding an oath from Loaysa. If she is the same maid, she has lost her concentration. She is less interested in the point of the oath than impressed by the form it has taken, the strangeness of which has caused her to muddle an oath with an incantation.

123. gregüescos: 'wide breeches'. See n. 93.

124. copete: 'quiff'; effeminate from a traditional viewpoint. 'El cabello que las damas traen levantado sobre la frente llamamos copete.... Por nuestros pecados hoy usan los hombres copete' (Covarrubias, under *copete*).

125. ¡Mal año para piñones mondados que más blancos ni más lindos sean!: *piñones:* edible pine kernels. 'You won't find peeled pine nuts whiter or prettier than those!' (Thacker).

126. pepitoria: A kind of poultry stew.

127. This song has been found in various contemporary versions. The gloss changes but the four-line *coplas* 'Madre, la mi madre...no me guardaréis' vary very little. See Eduardo M. Torner, *Lírica Hispánica. Relaciones entre lo popular y lo culto*, La lupa y el escalpelo, 5 (Madrid: Castalia, 1966), pp. 198-201. Cervantes used the same version (minus a stanza) in his *comedia La entretenida*, where it is sung and danced in an *entremés* that the servants stage for their masters. It is classified there as a *seguida*.

128. hiriendo de pie y de mano como si tuviera alferecía: 'flinging her feet and hands about as if she had epilepsy'.

129. cada una le dijo el nombre de las Pascuas: *Decirle a uno el nombre de las Pascuas:* to say insulting things about someone, to call someone names.

130. colores retóricos: 'rhetorical colours', a conventional name for 'rhetorical devices'. In Cervantes' day rhetoric was a studied art. Marialonso cannot have had any training in it but she may have a certain gift for it and Cervantes raises the possibility that she is directly helped by the Devil.

131. luengas y repulgadas tocas: 'long and hemmed toques [headdresses]'.

132. a esperar su contento de recudida: *de recudida*: an archaic phrase for *de rebote*. 'to await her turn for satisfaction' (Thacker).

133. encareciéndoles que debía de ser de momento: 'impressing upon them that it must be serious' (Thacker).

134. buenas entrañas: 'good wishes' or 'intentions'.

135. los casi ochenta míos: Carrizales was forty-eight when he went to the Indies and sixty-eight when he returned. He should now be approximately seventy, not almost eighty. Either he is exaggerating his age or Cervantes has made a slip.

136. lo tenga: *tenga gusto* (= *placer*).

137. transportados: 'unconscious'.

138. horras las esclavas y el negro: He gave the slaves their freedom. 'Horro. El que habiendo sido esclavo alcanzó libertad de su señor' (Covarrubias). Slaves were often freed in their masters' Wills.

139. despechado y casi corrido: 'angry and feeling almost insulted'.

140. dueñas de monjil negro y tendido y tocas blancas y luengas: '*dueñas* in their spreading nunnish black and long white toques'.

GLOSSARY

Argos: A character in Greek mythology with a hundred eyes. Surnamed 'Panoptes': 'All-seeing'.

bozal: A black slave who has only recently arrived in Spain and has little or no knowledge of the language.

cerradura de loba: See *llave de loba*.

estrado: A low, rug-covered platform where ladies sat on cushions, Moorish-style, to talk and receive visitors.

Indias, las: The contemporary name for Spanish America (also for Latin America in general), which had been thought by the early discoverers to lie in the Far East. This misunderstanding lies behind the name 'West Indies' still given to islands in the Caribbean.

ladino: A non-native Spaniard with a good command of the language. 'Al morisco y al extranjero que aprendió nuestra lengua con tanto cuidado que apenas le diferenciamos de nosotros, también le llamamos ladino' (Covarrubias, under *ladino*).

luego luego: straightaway.

luengo: long.

llave de loba: A key that fits a *cerradura de loba*: a spring lock that could not be opened from outside or inside without using the key. Probably called a *cerradura de loba* because it snapped into place, though Covarrubias has another explanation: its *guardas* or 'wards' (the indentations in a lock and its key) resembled the teeth of a wolf (under *lobado*).

matalotaje: A seafaring term meaning 'victuals' or 'provisions': 'La prevención de comida que se lleva en el navío o galera' (Covarrubias, under *matalotage*).

torno: A small encased turntable or revolving door normally found in convents and monasteries and used for delivering objects and messages from and to the outside world without the communicating parties seeing each other.

trompa de París: Jew's-harp: U-shaped and held between the teeth, with a central prong that is plucked.

velado: husband; groom.